"Remember that the use of the correct bait is half the battle."

Duncan's voice was as soft as the scent he had selected for her to wear.

"Is this all a lady needs to know of allure?" asked Alys.

"Certainly not. But we mustn't rush our fences. Slow and steady wins the race." He opened the door and peered along the corridor. "Come down to the library as soon as you are ready. A little mild flirtation might pique Mr. Pomeroy's interest."

"You wish me to conduct a dalliance with Mr. Pomeroy?"

He smiled at her as he stepped out into the corridor. "No, with me," he replied, disappearing before she could utter a suitable rejoinder.

Books by Coral Hoyle

HARLEQUIN REGENCY ROMANCE

Don't miss any of our special offers. Write to us at the following address for information on our newest releases.

Harlequin Reader Service
P.O. Box 1397, Buffalo, NY 14240
Canadian address: P.O. Box 603,
Fort Erie, Ont. L2A 5X3

THE ART OF THE HUNT

CORAL HOYLE

Harlequin Books

TORONTO • NEW YORK • LONDON
AMSTERDAM • PARIS • SYDNEY • HAMBURG
STOCKHOLM • ATHENS • TOKYO • MILAN
MADRID • WARSAW • BUDAPEST • AUCKLAND

This book is dedicated with love to my mother, Airel V. Hoyle, a woman of resiliency and tenacity, and to Christine Titus, for her inspiration

Women like not only to conquer, but to be conquered.
—William Makepeace Thackeray

Published August 1992

ISBN 0-373-31179-6

THE ART OF THE HUNT

PROLOGUE

Egypt, the Valley of the Kings, 1811

THE SETTING SUN'S last golden rays blessed the resting place of the long-dead pharaohs as another day closed. For thousands of years the blazing form of the ancient god Ra had departed in a grand show of light, disappearing in a flashing line of brightness. And so it continued unchanged.

Then, with the unbroken darkness that soon enclosed the Place of Truth, the quiet winds of night stole down the steep-walled canyon. A despairing sigh that spoke of past glories blew along the rugged crags and the hidden caverns.

This desolate valley of death rarely lured any living thing to venture into its eerie bounds; yet two stalwart souls cloaked in enveloping white robes entered cautiously. Though slowed by the intense blackness of night, the pair pressed on, pausing only when the wind murmured through the rock in humanlike whispers. The farther they went into the canyon the more courageous one seemed to become and the more hesitant the other appeared as he fell behind.

After a time, Baka, the leader, noticed the lagging steps of the younger man and seized him by the sleeve, forcing him to increase his pace. "Senusi," Baka said to his comrade, "by your fear you shame your father and his father...and all his fathers before him. You have turned from our ways in more than just your learning." He kicked up some sand, which was carried off by the wind. "An Egyptian does not quake at the sounds of the desert."

Senusi glanced about and pulled his silken robes closer, shivering from the cold and a mounting sense of apprehension. "This place is not of the desert. I know the desert and do not fear it. Tell me, do you believe the old stories? It is said that this valley of death is crossed every night by the great god Ra in his sacred barque. Only those worthy of passage can enter his boat." He gazed up at the cliffs. "The ancient kings have gone to their life beyond, but I am a mere man, and one who has been with many women. I wonder what Ra would do to me if he came?"

"Make you a eunuch." Baka laughed when Senusi instinctively bent forward and covered himself. "For many years you have been absent from our land, but our beliefs have never left you. Come, my friend! Kamose has sent for us and we must obey his command. Nothing will harm us, for our destiny has been decreed by the Roll of Fate."

Senusi looked at him dubiously. "You are most devout to the ways of the ancients. Though he is a great oracle, Kamose is not acknowledged as the rightful vizier of Upper and Lower Egypt. But still you obey him.''

''I obey him because he *is* the vizier, by right and inheritance. The Greeks, the Persians, the Romans and the Turks may in turn take our land and make us slaves, but they cannot steal away our customs if we hold them in our hearts.'' Though short in inches, Baka stood tall.

Slowly shaking his head, Senusi gave his leader a tolerant glance. ''Your world grows smaller with the passing of each year. The old ways are disappearing.'' He adjusted the fine cloth of his robe and drew himself up proudly. ''I have made much of what has been given me. Through my travels I have seen many things and my world is large. But you have never journeyed beyond Cairo. My cousin, who waits these many years to be your wife, says that you have sworn an oath on the souls of your fathers to live as they did.''

''I am the son of a royal guard. The kings are no more, but still I will serve and protect them until death claims me. Then I will stand guard in the world beyond.''

''You are too noble, Baka! There is much more than duty in this life to give a man purpose and pleasant days...and nights.'' Senusi peered from side to side, hoping that the old tales of the gods would prove to be wrong. If Ra did indeed take the souls of men up in his boat and carry them away, there would be many, many women who would mourn the loss of such a one as Senusi. He must live for the sake of all womankind. "I enjoy the heated whispers of a warm-skinned woman more than the cold moanings of death."

Baka cast him a sneering glare. "You think too much of women."

"You think too little of them! My cousin's womb will remain as barren as the desert for want of seed." Senusi swept back his robes, revealing his richly worked caftan. Then, with the swagger of an expert, he placed his fists on his hips. "A warrior who has never conquered a woman has not fought his best battle."

"Enough! Never allow your loins to overrule your mind." Baka turned and led the way along the floor of the canyon. "Come," he ordered over his shoulder, "the vizier must not be kept waiting."

As they trudged onward the moon appeared over the crest of the cliffs, casting silvery light into the canyon. The night's illumination reflected off the sand and the rock, making the valley as bright as noonday. With their way thus lit, Baka and Senusi soon found the designated place of their secret meeting. At a strange configuration of rocks, shaped like a pair of lions in repose, they stopped.

Gazing up at the cliff behind them, Baka said, "My father told me that this is the place where the first Ramses lies."

Senusi looked at their stark surroundings. "I have never doubted the word of your father, but I see no signs of a tomb."

"You were not meant to see," a quiet voice said from behind them. "The greatest artisans and craftsmen laboured long and hard to keep the burial place unknown." A man stooped by age slowly advanced upon them, then tossed back the hood of his robe. The ancient emblem of his high position hung about his neck.

Baka fell to one knee and bowed his head. After a moment of hesitation, Senusi reluctantly did the same.

"Kamose," Baka uttered reverently, "we have come to do your bidding. Command and it will be done."

After seating himself on an elevated outcrop of stone, Kamose spread his robes and held his walking staff like a sceptre of office. "Rise, Baka and Senusi. Here in this Place of Truth I must look into your souls, for only a man who is brave and loyal can be trusted with what I have to impart." He gazed long and hard at Senusi, until the younger man could no longer sustain so intense a stare. "Women and riches! It is as the Roll of Fate has foretold. Beware, young Senusi, you seek a life that is not of our ways. You wish to forget your heritage and your people. You want to be one with those who live beyond our sea. Your skin is light and your speech soft and learned. It is for this reason I have called you home.

"You have travelled among those who call themselves wise." The vizier stroked his beard thoughtfully. "You thirst for the water that will quench your need to know the mysteries of man. Knowledge without truth is an empty cup, Senusi. You yearn to be filled, but not for the good of your people do you do this." He thumped Senusi's chest with the staff. "You have ever been one to learn. It has been so since you were old enough to leave your mother's side. And you are clever. But are you a loyal Egyptian? To this you will soon find the answer, for you must serve... or disgrace your father."

Senusi's face deepened in colour, and he struggled within himself. Shame his father—never! "I will do as Kamose, the wise vizier, instructs me." He stepped back, bowing.

"Baka, my faithful one, come nearer." Kamose beckoned him forward. "If all the sons of Egypt had but a little of your zeal and willingness to serve we could overthrow those rulers who have come from distant lands. The Mamelukes were the lords for many, many years; then came the French, followed by the English, and now we have Mohammed Ali as the pasha of Egypt. *Pasha!*" He spat on the ground. "A Turkish title for one who beheads."

"We may yet return to power," Baka said solemnly, "if the gods will it." His earnest demeanour conveyed that he truly believed such a wondrous event could come to pass.

Kamose shook his head sadly. "Fate has been against us. We have been in bondage in our own land for over two thousand years. I, the rightful vizier, must receive you at night in a nearly forgotten valley. We continue our fathers' ways in secret." Raising his staff, he touched Baka's shoulder with it. "Bow, oh son of the faithful guard."

Baka obeyed him.

"I make you," Kamose said, in a loud, carrying voice, "Most Noble of the Noble, leader of our secret royal guard. Arise, Noble Baka!" He motioned for Senusi to come forward. "You must honour the Noble Baka. Obey him in all things."

Senusi looked with astonishment at his new commander. Grudgingly, he saluted him.

Rapping a rock for their attention, Kamose beckoned them to sit at his feet. "Senusi, your longing for what is beyond our lands will be of help to us. When you were a stripling you helped that man of learning at that place—"

"*L'Institut de l'Egypt,*" Senusi said, his eyes shining with the memories of his youth.

"The Frenchman Bonaparte wanted us all to believe he would make our land better and our people happier." Kamose scowled.

Senusi hung his head and murmured, "I believed his promises."

"But I was not deceived," the vizier replied. "What I must now tell you is most secret and is never to be repeated. More than ten years ago the French found a large black stone." Kamose paused to vaguely indicate its dimensions with a sweep of his hands before adding, "It is a most important stone. The English took it from the French. They call it the Rosetta Stone. You do not know of this stone. It was prepared long, long ago. On it are the texts that can help any who understand them to read the writings of the ancient ones. With this knowledge no tomb or sacred place will be safe from the grave robbers."

"Would not Ra protect the pharaohs?" Senusi asked in a cynical tone, but he glanced around as if afraid he might yet see a mystical boat come down through the valley.

"Silent rock sentinels stand guard over the tombs," Kamose said in a low voice, "and the sands of many thousands of years hide their entrances, but the wicked and the greedy have broken many of the seals of the pyramids. The invaders of our land have grown rich with the treasures of our pharaohs. Nothing in Egypt is safe. The great Sphinx of Pharaoh Chephren, now nearly covered by sand, was fired upon by the Mamelukes for cannon practice."

A rumbling sound came from Baka.

"I understand your anger, Noble Baka," said Kamose, "but there is little we can do to keep the invaders from plundering our land. Yet the Roll of Fate has decreed that we *must* protect the kings so their afterlife will not be troubled. It is our sacred duty."

Baka nodded his assent. "The spirits of the kings would become angered," he said in a voice that trembled with his own outrage, "if they were disturbed in their eternal rest."

Quelling the warrior with a glance, Kamose continued, "I entrust you with this mission: to bring back the Stone or, if it must be, destroy it. But be warned that many before you have failed and never returned to our land. The place where you will find the Stone is across the great sea in the city called London. The sun shines very little there. Ra must be cursing the English for taking the Stone."

Senusi thought upon the vizier's words, then muttered to himself, "If Ra has made the English lesser men, then their women will be wanting a virile man." He grinned expectantly, anticipating a lecherous future. "Oh, wise vizier, how can we carry out this deed?"

"You must trust the gods to show you the way," replied Kamose, "for it is written, 'In a far country you shall find treasure.' Be like the Nile while in that strange land. The Nile is silent, seeming to have no certain current. Moving gently, it embarks on a great journey. But to help you on your true course I will give to you, Senusi, a Roll of Fate, which will direct you in all things." He motioned for the two young men to rise. "Go now and do my bidding."

Baka stood and raised his arms to the night sky. "I vow to bring back the Stone!"

Stepping away, Senusi silently cursed the zealous Baka and then made a promise to Ra that if the god left him with all his important parts he would do his duty. But England was far away...and how would they ever find the Rosetta Stone in that sunless land? More importantly, were the women there a feast for the eye or could only a blind man find joy among them?

CHAPTER ONE

England, Twickenham, Middlesex, 1812

THE SPRING SUNLIGHT reflected softly on the Thames as that distinguished river flowed past a country villa. Gracing a rise which overlooked the waterway, Green Hill House reposed between two stands of large black walnut trees. The gentle setting and the harmonious surroundings had tempered the passage of time upon the unpretentious Palladian villa, giving it a much younger appearance than its one hundred years.

Situated near London, the villa had been originally bestowed upon a lady of renowned charms by a grateful monarch. The enterprising mistress then bequeathed the property to her great-nephew, who in turn bequeathed it to his nephew, Viscount Sommerville, a sober young lord. Though endowed with a past, Green Hill House eventually overcame its shadowy repute by being converted to a gathering place for learned men.

Sommerville—an important member of the House of Lords and the Society of Antiquaries—regularly brought his family to the villa before the start of each

Season. Though the establishment was not a major property of his lordship, still it was greatly loved by Sommerville and his family, and here they entertained frequent guests.

On this fine spring day, a small but select group of gentlemen strolled from the villa down the gently sloping lawn towards the river's edge. Lord Sommerville's third cousin, Giles Pomeroy, led the way, expounding like a lecturing don. Sommerville and his closest friend wandered behind the trio scarcely heeding Pomeroy's words.

"I needn't tell you gentlemen," Mr. Pomeroy said, "how vitally important this stone is to those of us who study the ancients. I know I needn't remind you how grateful we should be to my esteemed relative and patron, Lord Sommerville. It is through his prodigious influence, and the providential renovations being made upon the Egyptian Exhibit, that we are granted the rare privilege of a private study for an entire fortnight." He inclined his head graciously towards his third cousin. Then, with equal reverence, he bowed to the tawny-skinned man who walked close by his side. "Signore Senusi, how very fortunate we are to have you with us. Your letters of recommendation and your credentials can only add to the standing and credit of our humble assemblage. As I have often told Lord Sommerville, your arrival was a godsend."

Senusi glanced back at his attendant, the ever-present Baka, and smiled. Taking Pomeroy's arm, he said, "I must again express my gratitude for his lordship's kindness. To take a stranger into his house with such good fellowship is the mark of a great gentleman. I pray only that my efforts for the stone shall prove rewarding."

"I know we can depend on your expertise," Mr. Pomeroy replied, then continued to speak volubly with the two foreigners.

"That I misdoubt," murmured Sommerville's tall friend, who followed along with his lordship. Not only did the gentleman's height lend him distinction, his north country dialect did as well. "'Tis like setting the fox to guard the hens."

Sommerville, a man just past his thirty-sixth year and of average inches, gazed up at his crony. "I've asked you to be still upon that subject, Duncan," his lordship said in a low voice. "You must cease troubling Signore Senusi with your questions. Pomeroy says that your enquiries have disconcerted the Italian and interrupted their work."

"This study means much to you, Ned." Duncan frowned and paused thoughtfully. "But a man must follow his instincts. Mine tell me not to trust this fellow and his servant. However, this I promise: I will do my best not to intrude further upon the . . . ah, scholars."

"His credentials have satisfied Pomeroy and that must be the end of it. Besides, we've more important matters to concern us." Sommerville pulled out his timepiece as they neared the embankment. "Where is she? Alys is so competent in all other aspects of her life, why must she be forever arriving behind time? It matters not where she goes, she is always late. Confounded female, she must know how anxious her sister and I are for her arrival."

Duncan glanced over at Giles Pomeroy, who paced on the embankment. "It appears you are not the only one who awaits her coming with the greatest anticipation. Our scholar displays a nervous expectancy. 'Tis unnatural for one of his stoic nature. I'm curious. You've often said that your sister-in-law is most unusual, but is she a great beauty?"

ALYS CHAMPION SAT atop a crate on the bow of a gleaming new canal boat. The breeze fluttered the plumes in her Persian blue bonnet and the wisps of fine blond hair that framed her face. A dreamy expression softened her customary look of self-possession. Although an awning had been erected for her comfort, in her present state she did not seem to mind when the late-afternoon sunlight played across her face.

In a pensive tone, she asked a boatman for a cushion. Her comely lady's maid placed it for her and then curtsied in an exaggerated manner, enquiring if she desired anything else.

"Some cool water, if you please," Alys replied, assuming a playfully haughty pose.

With a pert smile, the abigail looked over the side of the boat into the Thames, then back at her mistress, seeming to speculate upon some unknown form of deviltry.

"To drink, you wretch," Alys said, fighting an inclination to laugh. It was futile to put on superior airs with her maid. The woman had known her for far too long to be squelched.

"A good dousing in cold water is said to be an excellent cure for the blue devils," said the maid as she gazed over the bow. "We're nearly there, Miss Alys. That's Richmond ahead and, as I recollect, around the bend is Green Hill House." She drew a bottle from the valise at her side. "I've some wine if you're thirsty." At her mistress's negative response, she shoved the bottle back and pulled out a fan. Waving it briskly over Miss Champion, she said, "This is a queer way for a lady to travel, I must say. A carriage is the proper conveyance for a lady of Quality."

"Proper, but dull. I'm in danger of becoming a predictable, fusty ape leader." Alys stood and moved to the low rail of the boat. "Today I rather feel like royalty. If I close my eyes…I can see myself sailing up the Nile under wind-filled sails with a galley full of slaves at the oars, rowing to the beat of a drum. My attendants would see to my every whim—even fresh water—for I am Queen of the Nile." She moved back to the crate and settled herself regally on it. "My

throne, as well as my headdress, would be of gold.''
She touched her bonnet.

The maid shook her head despairingly. "All that
wealth and beauty would be wasted if you're alone.''

"Men would fall at my feet to honour and . . . love
me. Then, when I could not favour them, they would
embark on a great crusade, performing many brave
deeds.''

"They did fall at your feet, for a time, and you sent
them away,'' the maid remarked. "If no one's been
paying you court, who's to blame?''

"Emma, you saucy minx, remind me to discharge
you. I really must find a more conformable woman to
serve me.''

"You've been trying to find one for these last ten
years, as long as you've been trying to find a husband
and with as much luck, too.''

A soft, inner light began to glow in Alys's azure
eyes.

"Now, don't you be thinking of that Mr. Pomeroy
again. It's blind you are to every gentleman save him.''
Emma clicked her tongue, but refrained from saying
another word on the subject.

Alys sighed. How like Emma to know even her most
cherished secret. But were her sentiments so obvious?
For eight years, since she was nineteen, she'd kept
hidden her deep regard for Giles Pomeroy. Since the
first moment she saw him, she had felt sure that she
could give her heart to no other. Unhappily, she'd not

had many opportunities to further her acquaintance with him. He'd been a Cambridge scholar then, and she'd thought she would have to wait only a short while for him to achieve his deserved good fortune and fame, that he would soon be free to turn his attentions towards her. But the passing years had begun to mock her. None the less, she'd remained constant to the fondest dreams of her heart.

Giles was her ideal in every way. His mind was far superior to that of the beau or the sporting gentleman. His strong sense of propriety gave decided order to his life, and his knowledgeable opinions upon various subjects made him a man to be revered and respected. Added to all these virtues was a visage marked by an unceasingly thoughtful expression. His low, thick brows imparted the look of a thinker. And she did admire a man with a ready mind.

If only he had the perception to see that she had formed a lasting passion for him.

She felt sure that he held a particular fondness for her. She wouldn't have waited all those years without some hope of happiness. No doubt it was his gentlemanly restraint that kept him from declaring his tendre.

Sommerville had written that Giles was very pleased about the prospect of her arrival. She could envision their blissful reunion and smiled in anticipation.

Alys tucked the few wisps of escaping hair under her bonnet and freshened the folds of the bow beneath her chin as the canal boat rounded the bend after Richmond. Seeing the cluster of gentlemen who awaited her, she felt the excitement mounting. Giles stood on the embankment, beckoning the boat to draw over to the shore. He was eager for her presence, of that she had no doubt. Her heart began to beat faster.

The boatmen released the tow lines, let the vessel drift for a moment, then punted until they finally reached the shallow water, where they prepared to dock. The moment the gangplank touched ground, Giles bounded up it.

"Miss Champion, you are here at last!"

Her heart beat wildly. He looked ready to embrace her. With a welcoming smile, she rose from the crate, and his eyes brightened.

He took a few steps towards her, then fell to his knees. With the most tender of caresses, he stroked the crate.

The crate! Her hopes dropped within her.

"It has arrived undamaged," he exclaimed in a relieved tone. His short fingers combed back his flowing, brown hair, leaving it in wild disarray. It was obvious that he had no interest in anything beyond the crate and its contents.

No, the crate was not damaged, but Alys felt that her heart had received a stunning blow. Her eyes burning with tears, she stared fiercely at Emma in a manner that dared the woman to utter just one disparaging remark.

Emma bustled about her mistress, dusting down her pelisse. The abigail's fussing was almost as unbearable as her unspoken pity. "Come, Miss Alys, you'll be wanting to rest after this ordeal. I'm meaning the journey," the maid added with a glance at Mr. Pomeroy. "I'll see to the baggage. You go ahead, miss."

Coolly raising her chin, Alys bid Mr. Pomeroy a good afternoon and proceeded to disembark. She whisked by Sommerville, who'd come aboard to greet her, and started to make her way unaided down the narrow plank. Her head held high, she felt rather than saw the edge of the board and wobbled as she neared the midway point. Her very next step seemed to find no footing, just an airy pause.

For a moment she teetered on one foot. Glancing down, she swayed towards the water. Just as she cried out, sure she was in for a dousing, a pair of hands clasped her roughly about the waist and swung her round. A large, dark-haired man, who had the broad shoulders of a field worker, finally set her down on the shore as if her five feet and eight inches were nothing to him. His gaze wandered over her in silent appraisal.

"Does she fare well, Duncan?" Sommerville called from the top of the gangplank.

"Aye, she'll do," he replied, tipping up her chin to see her face more fully.

His lively blue eyes disconcerted her. Was he inwardly laughing at her?

With as much composure as she could muster, she extended her gloved hand to her rescuer. "I daresay I should thank you...and I do. My abilities in the water are doubtful. Your quickness saved me from an..." She was about to say "from an excellent cure for the blue devils," but she wished to retain some shred of equanimity. "From a thorough dousing. I should have watched my step."

"It is said that nothing can be done both hastily and prudently. I am Duncan Todd," he said, bowing, "at your service...whenever you've a need, Miss Champion."

The soft sound of his rolling *r*s caught her fancy, and she felt herself put at a disadvantage. Adding to her disquiet was the decided twinkle in his eyes when he appended that "whenever you've a need." But she only had a moment to consider the matter, for Sommerville joined them and formally presented Alys to Mr. Todd and another gentleman, Signore Senusi.

His lordship, Edmund Pomeroy, the fourth Viscount Sommerville, who was not known for displaying his familial affections, merely pecked the back of her hand before placing it atop his arm. She smiled at his stiffness of manner as he led her up to the house. She had often wondered if, like herself, he kept his emotions hidden for a reason, or whether he was just a cold fish of a fellow.

In contrast to her brother-in-law, Signore Senusi was effusive with his particular attentions. Falling in be-

side her, he said, "Miss Champion, permit me to remark upon your regal beauty. Your fair hair can only
be matched by the glory of the noonday sun."

"He's Italian," murmured Sommerville as if an explanation were needed.

She smiled good-naturedly at the tawny-skinned
gentleman. "How kind of you, Signore Senusi. An
Englishman is not so very free with his compliments,
and we ladies do enjoy a well-turned phrase. I daresay Lady Sommerville has found your company quite
pleasing."

"Alas, I've been most disconsolate, for her ladyship has been keeping to her rooms of late. But now
that you are here, Miss Champion, I feel my spirits
beginning to rise. You must pardon if I stare, but such
rose-petal skin is—"

"Is quite common among English ladies," she interjected, sensing a change in Sommerville at the
mention of her sister's isolation. She leaned towards
her brother-in-law. "How does Thea fare?" she whispered.

"She tires very easily these days. Dr. Wingate insists that she remain in her rooms." Sommerville
sighed heavily and frowned, his brow furrowing.

In all the years that Alys had known her brother-in-
law, he had never displayed any outward sign of emotion. His restrained demeanor was renowned. Indeed, this was one reason he was so effective as a
diplomatic aide.

His unusual show of concern alarmed her. "Edmund, what is it? You must tell me." She led him away from Senusi.

"Dr. Wingate will not allow the girls in to see their mother...says they upset her unduly. Yet Thea worries so about them when they are withheld from her. And...and she wants very much to see them, for she has had some dreams that have frightened her." His frown deepened with the length of his pause. "As her time draws near, she fears that she will not survive her travail."

"My poor Thea. Take me to her at once, Sommerville. I should have come sooner."

Sommerville led her over the terrace and through the Great Room, then up the marble staircase to the master's suite of rooms. "I daresay you tire of being at the beck and call of all your relations," he remarked as they neared Thea's bedchamber.

"Did you not know that a spinster's lot is to become a boil on the backs of her relations? Just when they think they are rid of her, she rises again to give them the devil of a time." She stripped off her gloves and removed her hat before entering the door that Sommerville held open for her. She took a few steps, then stopped to grope her way forward, for the room was shrouded in darkness. "Thea?" she asked, in a hushed voice.

"Alys? Are you there? Where are you?"

Following her sister's voice and the rustle of sheets, Alys found her way to Thea's bed and felt for her sister's hand.

"Come closer, Alys. I cannot see you," Thea said fretfully.

"Does the light give you the headache?"

An impatient sigh escaped from Thea. "You know I am scarcely ever sick, but I've not been sleeping well at night. And then I did the silliest thing—I dozed off during tea. Sommerville thought I had fainted and sent for the physician. Dr. Wingate now insists that nothing disturb me, not even a glimmer of light."

"What nonsense! I do not mean to meddle, truly I don't, but what sort of quack has Sommerville got attending you?" Alys fumbled towards a wall and felt for a drapery, then pulled it back slowly. The afternoon's fading light filtered into the chamber, revealing the bed's delicate new hangings and Thea reclining on a bank of pillows. A very fetching lace cap adorned her fair head.

Alys went to her sister and embraced her tenderly. Then, moving back, she said, "You are too pale, my dear. But I am here now and shall soon have you in fine fettle. Do not trouble yourself to argue with me, Thea; my mind is set upon the matter. I should have come sooner. Sophy has a very good nursemaid, and I was scarcely needed. I daresay I was very much in the way."

"*I* have no doubt that Sophy, being the youngest, would have felt herself ill-used had I the indelicacy to call you here sooner. She cannot pick an ell of cloth without your advice, so how can you think she would find her way through an outbreak of measles? You should have been the eldest, not I. It is no use disclaiming, dear, dependable Alys. Your family cannot get along at all without you." Thea peeked up through her lashes at her husband, who stood just inside the door. "Can we, Sommerville?"

He gave no answer, yet seemed magnetically drawn towards his wife's bed. His eyes feasted upon Thea as if he hadn't partaken of her beauty in days.

On the pretense of letting in some fresh air, Alys relinquished her place beside Thea and moved to the window. Out of the corner of her eye, she watched as Sommerville placed a chair by the bed and sat down. His hand crept over the coverlet towards Thea's and hers moved towards his, but somehow their fingers never touched.

Alys noticed that they refrained from making contact. Each seemed to watch the other for a sign that neither would give. How could they have conceived four children and still be shy of each other? she wondered.

Pushing open the window, Alys breathed deeply as she tried to fathom the undercurrents passing between Edmund and Thea. "It's remarkable how much better one feels when the air is clear. I daresay you two have things to say to each other," she stated plainly, "and I must make sure my maid has not scorched all my gowns. I shall leave you now." She turned to go.

"No!" they both cried together, looking frightened of being left alone.

Alys leaned back against the pane and shook her head slowly. Was there ever a household in a sorrier state? Well, she must see what she could do to set things right; the thought of playing matchmaker for a married couple presented an appealing challenge.

A tingle of awareness crept up her spine and she straightened, her eyes widening. Why settle for making only one couple happy? Did she not have a duty to herself and Giles? Even though he'd wounded her pride, she still cared deeply for him. And who would see to their happiness if not she?

The prospect of settling everyone's affairs filled her with a sense of purpose that stimulated her. At times she wondered if perhaps she was becoming a managing female. Perhaps this propensity of hers to direct the lives of others had become too heady. Yet only when this indomitable urge rushed through her did she feel that she was living a truly worthwhile life.

Was it so terrible to be the sort of woman who liked to take charge? In dealing with Giles it was obviously imperative.

She knew that for at least a fortnight Giles would be residing under the same roof as she. With a little determination—and she was certainly determined—she might turn the situation very much to her advantage.

After all, she'd waited so long for him—dreamt so long of being his—she could not give up now. And since he was occupied with many important matters it behooved her to conduct, in his stead, the delicate manoeuvres that would culminate in matrimony. She would do the courting for him.

CHAPTER TWO

"OF ALL THE GENTLE ARTS that a lady is taught, why has she never been instructed in the delicate art of seduction?" Alys wondered aloud, as she scowled at herself in the peer glass. After critically considering the faint sprinkling of freckles on either side of her nose, she reached for the rice powder. "Surely that knowledge would be beneficial, would it not, Emma?"

The abigail never lacked for an opinion on any subject. "There's a certain sort of female who has the knowledge of how to capture a man. I believe a school is kept in Covent Garden for their kind."

Pausing in her application of powder, Alys remarked, "Never say that *you* attended such a school."

"Oh, no, miss. But my cousin, a very unfortunate girl, received a thorough—"

"Let us forgo your poor cousin's history, though I know it would have been fascinating to hear," she said with an appreciative smile. "The fruit of your family tree is always juicy. So many of your relatives have a dubious past. But I was speaking of the education of ladies of Quality. A knowledge of allure would—"

"Would ruin any woman with a claim to refinement. If ladies had such an education they wouldn't be ladies…as my cousin could attest," Emma added with a smirk of satisfaction. She picked up a comb and began to dress Alys's hair for the evening.

Alys retorted, "But without such knowledge, how is a lady to bring herself to a gentleman's notice?"

The maid eyed her suspiciously. "You're not still betwattled over that Mr. Pomeroy? Not after today!"

"That is none of your affair."

"Now, it's no use getting huffish with me, Miss Alys. I don't quake under those cool stares, not like some, I don't. And if it's a man you're wanting to attract you'd best not practise such looks. Men like their women to be soft and biddable." Emma clicked her tongue. "'Tis a great pity that your mama went to her eternal rest before you completed your come-out." She paused in her work to assume the matronly posture she always used when about to make an important or unusual statement. "A mother passes on all a lady's supposed to know concerning the finer points of flirtation and setting one's cap for a husband."

A small sigh of regret for missed opportunities escaped Alys's lips. "Mother also failed to instruct Thea in those finer points." She paused reflectively. "Poor Mama's health kept her from enjoying the pleasures of Society. Had it not been for Great-Aunt Etta, none of us girls would have even had our come-outs." She looked at her maid doubtfully. "But how do mothers know of allure?"

"How indeed!" Emma fiddled with a ribbon before twining it through Alys's hair. "Am I a mother? Am I supposed to know *how* they know? But, on this I vow, somewhere between a lady's wedding day and the first day of her daughter's come-out she's learned more than she ever knew in the schoolroom."

"Well, it is a great pity that fathers do not similarly instruct their sons on how to conduct a courtship. I believe men know nothing of how to woo a lady." The image of Giles caressing that blasted crate kept tormenting her.

"I've heard it said that when a man's affections are engaged he becomes very particular in his attentions," Emma said, using a cultured voice to add authority to her words. "I myself have upon many occasions—"

"If you boast again about your various conquests—the butlers, the valets, the coachmen—I promise to discharge you this very hour without a character."

Alys rose abruptly, angry with herself for saying such mean-spirited words. She knew that below stairs her own reputation for being cold was unfavourably compared to that of her maid, who was known for her over-generous nature with men. Emma actually seemed to enjoy her unmarried state. Though she was three years older than Alys and would soon be thirty, she appeared to find her life a constant adventure. Of course, the abigail usually received a declaration from each man who fell under the spell of her charms, but she'd refused every one, saying she'd not yet found her true love.

How odd that with the advantage of breeding and fortune, Alys had fared poorly compared to her maid.

"Forgive me, Emma. You are a treasure...one I would be loath to lose."

"Nothing to forgive. You're out of sorts, Miss Alys, and that's a fact. We both know you won't turn me out. Who else have you got to tell your doubts to other than me? Not those sisters of yours. In their eyes you're a perfect piece of work who's never wrong and has no troubles of your own." Emma helped Alys into her evening gown of deep blue silk. "There now, don't you look fine. It's always been a puzzlement to me why some gentleman hasn't snapped you up."

"I have neither your ample bosom nor my sister's soft disposition to tempt a man. I may be a spinster for a long while yet."

Emma draped a Norwich shawl over Alys's shoulders. "You're not so old you've got to settle for the likes of that Mr. Pomeroy."

"I'll have you know Mr. Pomeroy is a gentleman of distinction—a scholar. His opinions are sought by many. Even the Regent seeks his advice upon matters concerning Egyptian antiquities."

While holding the door open for Alys to pass through, Emma remained silent, but her arched brows gave mute testimony to her scepticism.

In the corridor, Alys paused. "You might as well speak. I can feel your words hanging on my back."

"That Mr. Pomeroy is a dunderhead—no matter his learning. He can't see what's under his nose. I'll wager, miss, that tonight he doesn't even notice you, or your lovely gown either."

Alys squared her shoulders. "I hope you can afford to lose a few shillings." She kicked the demi-train of her gown behind her, then walked away, ignoring as best she could the snigger coming from her brazen-faced maid. Just this once she would relish besting Emma.

LORD SOMMERVILLE PUSHED back his chair and stood. "Gentlemen, please continue to savour your port, but you must forgive me if I do not linger at table with you. My sister-in-law has ordered tea to be served in the library. Lady Sommerville will be awaiting us there." A look of worry passed over his face and he added, "I would not want to keep my wife from retiring early."

Duncan Todd shoved his half-emptied glass away, and waited for the other gentlemen to follow his lead. He noticed that the Italian was quite ready to forgo the company of the men for the pleasure of an evening spent with the ladies. Senusi had quickly gained a reputation with the housemaids, and Duncan wondered if the foreigner's romantic success would extend to higher climes—Miss Champion, perhaps.

Senusi's ability to cajole gentlemen was already proven. His success with Giles Pomeroy had been complete from the very first. But Pomeroy had been easily wooed; it took only a few respected names and official-looking seals to win him over. The scholar's fatal flaw was that he assessed a man's worth by the cachet he carried. Credentials and honours mattered more to him than a man's deeds and character.

To Duncan the height of Pomeroy's folly had come when the scholar favoured a cold hunk of stone over the comely Miss Champion. The crestfallen lady had scarcely maintained her dignity after receiving such a snub. And she'd tried so valiantly to hide her partiality for the scholar, but from some eyes nothing can be hidden. How sad it was to love someone and be disregarded.

He wondered what he could do to assist her in her plight. He glanced speculatively at Giles Pomeroy.

"Well, Mr. Pomeroy," Duncan said, lingering behind the others to wait for the ruminative gentleman, "it appears that there is an agreeable surprise awaiting us in the library. Shall we go?"

Tossing back his hair, Giles beamed happily. "Yes, a treasure worth more than gold." So saying, he rose and started for the door in a slow, deliberate gait. "I can scarcely wait to unveil her."

Duncan paused perceptibly before continuing to stroll along at Pomeroy's plodding pace. "Unveil her? Then I daresay that you are anxious to declare yourself and have the vows spoken."

"Declare myself? What vows? Sommerville told me nothing of this. The ceremony is to be quite simple."

"The banns have been posted then?"

"Bands? It is too late for restrictions. We shall not be stopped by anyone. She's come too far for that. She's an exquisite relic and I yearn to run my hands over her finely etched features."

Duncan caught hold of his laughter and struggled to contain himself. He had suspected they'd been speaking at cross-purposes, but to such an absurd end?

"Miss Champion *also* has finely etched features," Duncan remarked, thinking to draw her to the scholar's notice. "Blue eyes with a hint of a dream in them; hair the colour of sun-ripened wheat, but soft as a downy chick; and a chin so strong one knows she would stand by a man even in his darkest hour." He stopped, struck by his own words. "She is not at all the sort of lady who would suit you."

"Who, Mr. Todd? Were you speaking of someone?" Giles stared at him in bewilderment. "Really, sir, you north-countrymen have a habit of rambling in the most nonsensical manner. But I must confess that I am a man whose mind is very much occupied. I scarcely ever listen to twaddle." He paused in the library doorway until his gaze found the object of his hopes and dreams: the draped Rosetta Stone. He hurried over to it, catching the arm of Senusi and dragging him along in his wake. The manservant Baka silently followed behind and stationed himself at his master's shoulder.

Quietly Duncan observed Miss Champion. *Deep in her breast lives the silent wound,* he thought as she tried to cover her chagrin. He advanced towards her and she busied herself pouring a cup of tea.

"Might I be of assistance?" His glance indicated the tea, but his soft tone conveyed something more.

She smiled demurely. "Would you be so kind as to take this cup to my sister? Thank you, sir."

Duncan bowed, then turned away to fulfil his commission. He found Lady Sommerville by the fireplace, tucked into an open sedan-chair, the sort that is carried by lackeys. Sommerville stood beside her like a guard protecting the Crown Jewels.

"I am told there's to be an unveiling," Duncan remarked as he handed her ladyship the dish of tea.

Lady Sommerville hid her grin as she sipped her brew. "Dear Cousin Giles does so enjoy pomp and ceremony," she murmured. "Only see how he capers round that rock like a child about to receive a sweet. Sommerville, perhaps you should have him begin, before we are all infected with his excitement. I admit that I am curious to see the source of such great eagerness."

Sommerville consulted his timepiece and frowned. "He'd better get on with it. The hour is late."

"Late?" her ladyship questioned. "Why, it is not yet nine o'clock. If we were in Town—"

"Dr. Wingate says Town life would be most injurious to your health."

"Yet," her ladyship interjected before her husband could proceed, "see how good for me it has been to come down and join you. My spirits are ever so much lighter. Alys may not be versed in the arts of healing, but she does know how to chase away the blue devils. If only it weren't so late, then I might see my little girls."

"As for the late hour, my dear lady, you are to retire shortly." Sommerville cast his wife a stern, authoritative look before turning his attention to Pomeroy. "Giles, the ladies are anxious to see the Stone. Please proceed."

While Giles scrambled to place a chair for Senusi, Duncan escorted Miss Champion to a sofa which was positioned to give an excellent view of the spectacle.

Giles stepped next to the draped stone and cleared his throat. "Ladies and gentlemen," he began as he searched for something in his waistcoat, "I had a few words written down, but . . . they elude me at the moment." His brows dipped in thought. "I haven't a notion of where the paper can be." He peered at Sommerville and gestured helplessly. "Pray forgive me if my remarks are not as polished as they might have been. I am not a man gifted in elocution, yet the importance of this ceremony brings to my heart a rush of rhetoric. I believe it was Bacon who said, 'These times are the ancient times, when the world is ancient.' We live in an era when at last the edifying relics of a bygone age are prized and esteemed for their true worth.'' He paused to take a deep breath.

"Giles,'' Sommerville said in a low voice of warning as he tapped the face of his timepiece.

Giles pulled at his collar. "Yes, yes, as I was saying . . . it gives me great pleasure to present the antiquity for which we have waited so long. Ladies and gentlemen, the Rosetta Stone!'' He whisked the cover off and stood back, clasping his hands reverently to his breast. "Is she not a thing of beauty to behold?''

Senusi and Baka stared at the stone as if mesmerized.

A slab of black basalt, just over three feet long and two feet wide and nearly a foot thick, sat heavily upon a sturdy mangerlike support. Beneath the rock's cumbrous weight the floorboards seemed to groan.

The face of the Stone was covered with three different forms of writing, one having many symbols. Timorously, Giles reached out and ran his stubby fingers lovingly over a line of inscription.

Duncan glanced to the side to catch Miss Champion's reaction. She quickly replaced her initial expression of disappointment with a look of polite interest. "What is your opinion, Miss Champion?''

She gazed at him in surprise. "Did you ask my opinion, sir? You must forgive me if I stare, but I am unaccustomed to having a gentleman request my thought upon a subject other than needlework or water-colours."

"I meant no offence and cry pardon if I've overstepped the bounds of propriety. I'm j'st a north-country lout who knows n' better," he said, deliberately assuming the speech of an uncouth yeoman. "But I am curious. What d' you think of it?"

She looked at him with a wary expression, then gave her attention to the Stone and considered it for a time. "Do you wish my honest response, sir?"

Duncan slowly smiled. "Miss Champion, a man may search a lifetime for a woman who will give him an honest response, and here you sit ready to give it. Please, do be honest . . . and forgive me if *I* stare, for 'tis rare to encounter a lady who is without guile."

"Sir, guile is like the buckram in a gentleman's coat. It is worn, everyone knows it is there, but it is seldom discussed. How rare it is these days to encounter a gentleman without buckram." She grinned waggishly.

"I myself ne'er use it. M' tailor says I've the look of a yoked ox with it. Now, as for guile . . ." He returned her grin with one of impish innocence.

Her eyes widened in surprise and she gave him a closer look. "You are not at all like Sommerville's usual friends," she said quietly. Her tone carried a hint of bewilderment. "As for my opinion, I find the Stone rather disappointing." She peeked quickly at Giles as if to assure herself he hadn't overheard her remark. "Oh, I know it is of great worth, but it isn't at all what I thought it would be. Besides, it looks as if it is chipped at the corners."

Giles had moved back near them to survey the Stone from a broader perspective. "Chipped?" From his aggrieved expression one would think Miss Champion had blasphemed.

"I daresay she meant to say 'not completely whole,'" Duncan offered tactfully.

"Not completely whole?" Giles looked aghast, then perplexed. "What would you—a gentleman *farmer*—know of such things?"

"But it is obvious that large chunks of the Stone are missing," Alys interjected. "It has a most irregular shape."

"You, Miss Champion, defame her shape?" Giles appeared shocked. "As a scientist, I am duty-bound to refrain from making judgements which are rash and unfounded."

"But were not the Egyptians known for the symmetry of their structures?" asked Duncan.

Giles seemed mollified by this question. "Some of their columns and buildings are said to be very pleasing to the eye, but here we are speaking of a rock used for writings. You must concede that I would know more about these matters than you, Mr. Todd. After all, you are merely an *honorary* member of the Society of Antiquaries.'' He raked his hand through his hair as if perplexed. "And why a man devoted to sporting pursuits wishes to associate himself with that revered society passes the bounds of my ability to reason.''

"And of your ability to be civil.'' Sommerville stared at his cousin. "Duncan Todd is my friend…and my guest. Need I say more?''

Duncan went to Sommerville and, clapping him on the shoulder, said, "You always could be bearish when the need arose. But your growls may upset her ladyship. It was foolish of me to step in when Mr. Pomeroy was ready to go toe to toe with Miss Champion. You mustn't be cross with him, for I should have known better. A wise man never thrusts his sickle into another's corn.''

Sommerville frowned and seemed to consider the matter, but his good lady captured his attention by trying to suppress a wide yawn. "My lady, you should retire.''

"An excellent suggestion, Sommerville,'' said Miss Champion. "We shouldn't overspend her strength. Would you escort Thea to her chambers? I'll ring for the footmen.''

To the room at large, her ladyship said, "Pray excuse me if I bid you good-night at such an early hour, but my lord will have his way in this…and I must obey him. Good night, Alys. Good night, gentlemen.'' With

Sommerville leading the way, the footmen carried her out.

Miss Champion also excused herself, saying that she would leave the gentlemen to their examination of the antiquity. Gracefully slipping away from Senusi's effusive adieus, she murmured a good-night to all.

A short while later, Duncan found her by following the faint sound of music coming from the Great Room. There she sat at the pianoforte, softly playing a melancholy piece. He listened for a time and felt that he knew her state of mind. Ah, the poignant pangs of unrequited love.

As a sporting gentleman who'd been raised on his father's vast lands in Northumberland, Duncan knew that when approaching wild game he must stand downwind so as not to alert his prey to his presence. At the moment he viewed Miss Champion as a doe pausing to refresh herself. If he wished to get close he must proceed slowly and with great care. He must tread cautiously lest she dash for cover.

He moved as quietly as mist rolling over a moor. When at last she became aware of his presence she showed no sign of alarm, but went on playing. She seemed to accept him as a friendly intruder.

"Do you know anything of music, Mr. Todd?" she asked.

"Only that I like some of it and could live happily without hearing the rest."

"Are you truly a sporting gentleman?" She stopped playing and directed her unwavering gaze at him. "I had begun to find you an agreeable companion... until Mr. Pomeroy made his startling revelation."

He tried not to show his surprise. He'd thought better of her and was disappointed that she should judge a man by some trifling matter disclosed by another. "You find it startling that I am *merely* an honorary member of the Society of Antiquaries? I may not have the zeal and the devotion that Pomeroy has for relics, but I wish to learn of them and I enjoy the fellowship."

"The startling revelation I refer to, sir, is your passion for sporting pursuits."

"Passion? That's a strong word for a man's pastime."

She stiffened. "My father was just such a one as you: a man who favoured fox and field above all else. He was a complete enthusiast—fair weather or foul, it mattered not." She ended this statement with a wistful sigh. "He continued to follow the hounds until an inflammation of the lungs laid him to rest in his beloved sporting field. I have no high opinion of men who worship sport, sir."

"You should not set your mind against a gentleman merely because he favours something you loathe. The knowledge of an angler or pugilist or hunter could benefit even a lady. Since I have the skills of all three

I am amply qualified to be of assistance to you, Miss Champion.''

"What nonsense! Your boast is empty." She glared at him. "What assistance could you render?"

Slowly, purposefully, he advanced upon her and leaned over the pianoforte, boldly coming face to face with her. "I've watched you. Your composure hides from some your uncertainty of mind. Your peevish nature is probably due to your continued state of spinsterhood. Babes seem to gentle a woman—at least it was so with my sisters. Perhaps you worry that you may never make a suitable match and have children of your own."

For a moment only, she looked at him as if he had revealed her most guarded secret. Then she raised her chin and stared coolly, defiantly at him.

How brave, but stubborn she was. He wanted to relent, yet could not. "A lady like yourself might think to settle for what is closest at hand. She might even fancy herself in love with someone like Mr. Pomeroy."

Her eyes widened with a startled look.

Unrelentingly, he continued, "But what can she do? There are many things a proper lady of Quality knows, but how to trap her quarry is not one of them. That is something a sporting gentleman knows. A proud lady would disdain to learn. A brave, sensible woman would venture. Which sort are you, Miss Champion? Might I instruct you in the art of the hunt?"

CHAPTER THREE

ALYS ROSE FROM HER PLACE at the pianoforte, her emotions warring within her. How dare he be so bold as to offer her instruction—and upon such a delicate topic? What presumption! He had trampled the rules of propriety by speaking so bluntly. Mercilessly, he had cut her to the quick. Yet she sensed his intent was not to inflict pain, but rather to prick her consciousness as deeply as needed to gain her attention. She was hurt, but with the hurt came hope. Could he instruct her in those stratagems she'd not learned from her mother? Did he indeed know the secrets of the art of the hunt?

"I will grant," she said, walking away from him, "that you are probably an expert in sport, but how does your expertise extend itself to the drawing-room? You have not yet convinced me that your words are nothing more than an idle boast."

He followed three paces behind her, giving her just enough distance. "Would I be too brash if I expounded upon a subject that is discussed in the clubs, but never in drawing-rooms?"

She indicated that he should proceed.

"Consider the nature of sport. Most gentlemanly pastimes involve skill and struggle—man against man, or man against nature. Some scholars contend that the civilized gentleman pursues sport rather than making war." He paused thoughtfully. "These learned men also espouse the theory that the stratagems and policies of love and war are alike."

She glanced back at him, letting her scepticism show.

"You needn't look at me with such disbelief. Those are the theories of philosophers." He smiled engagingly at her. "The men of learning, whose words you obviously value, say that love and war and sport are much the same. Since I am an authority on sport, clearly you must accept me as an expert in the other fields as well."

His words had the ring of logic, yet why was she so confused? "I'll grant that you are a master sly-boots, sir."

"But what have you to lose by throwing in your lot with a cunning sportsman?" Circling round her, he scrutinized her. "Haven't you the courage to venture?"

She raised her chin defiantly.

"Are you afraid of me, Miss Champion?"

"Should I be?" She felt only a little fearful. Never had she considered relinquishing such a degree of command to another. Actually she was more wary than frightened. Mr. Todd was certainly not some country bumpkin set loose in the metropolis. "As a woman of sense, I foresee many hazards should I fall in with your scheme." Her brow creased as she thought. Could she trust a man who was nearly a stranger? She gazed into his blue eyes—such earnest eyes—and decided. "As I have no plan of my own, consider me your pupil, sir."

He took her hand and bowed over it. "I promise you, Miss Champion, that you shall have your heart's desire—even the one that is most deeply hidden. And I never promise more than I can perform. In my family I am known as . . . the knight errant," he said with a rueful grin. "And as your fellow conspirator, I shall guard your confidences well; they shall be as secret as the grave."

"My mother would undoubtedly sit up in her grave, God rest her soul, could she know that I have placed my trust in a sporting gentleman. Father gave her no end of grief with his pursuits." She moved away from him with a flick of her demi-train, as if she still couldn't accept him. "If you are to instruct me, when do my lessons begin?"

"Slow and steady wins the race, as *my* mother always says. She's seen four of my sisters through their come-outs and is presently popping off the youngest of the brood."

"I wish my. . ." Alys sighed wistfully. "It matters not now. I daresay you shall have to do. Though I would have preferred the advice of your mother."

"Mother would tell you to trust me with all your heart. Whatever the future holds, nothing is impossible to a willing heart."

Quite taken by surprise, she gazed at him in astonishment. How could he know that very saying had always been her personal motto? Did men of a sporting nature possess these inexplicable powers? "Mr. Todd, you are a remarkable man."

"Whist, now. You must save your flattery for Mr. Pomeroy," he said, wagging a finger at her. "Besides, I'm just an ordinary farmer, whose knowledge comes from observing nature. My father, Lord Foxton, believes that a man can learn more about his fellow creatures outdoors than when closed in a schoolroom."

"Your father is also a sportsman?" She winced inwardly as she wondered how far back his strain of sporting blood ran.

He frowned. "Father would take offence should anyone be unwise enough to call him a sportsman. He considers Whips and Knowing Ones to be frivolous fellows who fritter their time away on empty occupations. One of his greatest pleasures is to stride out across our lands with a dog at his side." A look of esteem and affection softened his expression. "In Northumberland, my father is well respected."

Though he'd gently chastised her, Alys viewed Duncan with admiration. "Would that we could all say the same of our fathers." She clutched her hands together and looked down. "I believe you may teach me much I haven't known. Until tomorrow, then." She wanted to escape from the awkwardness she felt. Hastily she turned to go.

He caught her at the door and tucked her hand into the crook of his arm. "As conspirators, we must part on better terms than this, Miss Champion. I shall escort you to your chamber while you enumerate the many virtues of Mr. Pomeroy."

She didn't comply, but remained silent, feeling embarrassed to speak aloud the thoughts she'd kept hidden for so long.

As they took the stairs, Duncan said, "No doubt you favour his height, it being so near your own. I daresay you would make a charming pair in a country dance."

"I cannot ever recall seeing Mr. Pomeroy doing a set of figures. He always seems to be occupied with something much more important—his antiquity work, you know."

"You enjoy music. Perhaps the two of you have sung a duet together?"

"No." Curiously she found herself wondering if Duncan's voice, with its rolling *r*s and deep timbre, would lend itself well to song. Giles, she suspected, possessed a fine tenor. She felt sure he must have the same fondness for music as she, for his mind was so refined and cultured.

"And children . . . is he fond of them?"

She glanced at him, annoyed by the stream of questions she could not answer. How did one casually bring up the subject of children with a scholar?

"Now see what I've done: here I was striving to make amends and I've only succeeded in making you a cross-patch."

She could not withstand the twinkle in his eyes. "Cross-patch, indeed," she said with a grudging smile.

"Ah, that's better. We are on the road to becoming fast friends. Of course, to be true friends we must address each other by our Christian names. It would be agreeable if you were to call me Duncan. And might I address you as—"

"Alys," interjected a small voice from behind them. "*Aunt* Alys." Perched on the steps which led up to the floor of the schoolroom sat a very young girl in her night-gown. She wiped a tear from her cheek and then pulled the hem of the gown over her bare toes. "Nobody kissed me good-night—not for days and days." Another tear streaked down.

Alys scooped the child up and held her tightly. "Nelly dear, what are you doing from your bed?"

"I want my mama," the three-year-old replied in a quavering voice. "Aunt Alys, where's my mama? Did she die?"

A rush of emotions left Alys bereft of speech. She looked to Duncan for help.

"Nelly, is it?" he asked, taking her little hand in his. "If I were to guess, I would say you're all of four years old."

Alys glanced at him, surprised to find that he knew it was a form of flattery to add a year or two to a child's age.

The flaxen-haired little girl peeked up at him from under her nightcap. "You're a big man. I'm this many." She held up three dimpled fingers. "One, two, three."

Alys pushed down the lump in her throat. "Mr. Todd, may I present Miss Eleanor, whom we affectionately call Nelly."

"A great honour, Miss Eleanor," Duncan said, bowing. "Did you know that your papa and I are fast friends? I've visited here many times, but why have I never seen you?"

"The mean dragon keeps us upstairs. She says little girls don't pester the—the guests," Nelly said, working to pronounce the last word. "Where is Mama, Aunt Alys?"

"You mustn't worry about your mama, my lamb. The doctor said she had to rest, but she'll see you soon. I promise." Alys calmly sustained Duncan's incredulous look.

"As I remember," he murmured, "Dr. Wingate has forbidden visits from the children."

"Please believe there are many things I can manage on my own." Alys smiled confidently. "Nelly, tomorrow—after tea—you'll see your mama. But now we must put you back into bed."

Nelly wrapped her arms around Alys's neck. "Don't let the dragon get me."

"Miss Nelly, forgive me if I boast," Duncan said in gallant tones, "but I am a very fine hunter, and dragons are what I hunt best. Shall we see if I can tame this dragon of yours?"

Silently Nelly nodded, but still she held on to Alys.

"Have you ever ridden on the back of a charger?" Duncan asked, gently taking Nelly from Alys. He swung Nelly up onto his shoulders, where she clung to him by wrapping her arms about his head, just over his eyes. "Your charger must see to mount the steps, little one." When she grasped his cravat for reins, he laughed and shrugged in resignation.

Alys followed him up the steep stairs, holding the rail with one hand and the front of her gown with the other. She marvelled at the ease with which he balanced her niece.

"Shall we slip her back in so the dragon never knows she was gone?" Duncan asked in a whisper as he reached the top of the stairs. "I'd face the dragon in its den, but as I recall, dragons have a sly way of striking back at the unprotected. And she's such a little girl to brave a serpent's retribution."

Alys led the way down the narrow corridor to a chamber situated between the nanny's room and the schoolroom. "The girls sleep in here." She slowly opened the outer door and peeked in. Three beds were placed a sufficient distance from one another as to discourage any exchanges at night between the sisters. All was quiet, except for a rhythmic sort of growl coming from behind the connecting door. "Nanny Jinks," Alys whispered, pointing to the door, "the dragon."

After lifting Nelly off his shoulders, Duncan knelt down and kissed her hand. "It's been an honour to serve you, dear lady," he whispered. "Sweet dreams."

Nelly took Alys by the hand and led her aunt to her little bed in the corner. Tucking her niece in, Alys noticed once again the plainness of the furniture and roughness of the woollen blankets—very Spartan for a viscount's children. "Tomorrow, I promise," Alys murmured as she leaned over to kiss the little girl's cheek, "you will see your mother."

As Alys turned to leave she saw Duncan stealthily treading across the room to the connecting door. He eased it open and listened. Hurrying to his side, she tried to pull him away, until her own curiosity overcame her better judgement. She peered in. There lay Nanny Jinks, clutching her hands together over her chest as if uttering a constant prayer through the night. But the sounds that came from between her clenched teeth were hardly reverent, for they were akin to the growls of a mad dog.

"The dragon sleeps," Duncan whispered in Alys's ear.

When his breath touched her skin she jerked back from him, startled by the tingle that passed from her ear down her neck.

Out in the corridor, she kept her distance from Duncan. He didn't seem to notice her caution. He merely released a sigh of relief as they began to descend the stairs. "'Tis curious for Ned and her ladyship to have such a dragon in charge of the welfare of their girls."

"Most of Thea's servants were chosen by the dowager. Nanny Jinks was the dowager's latest piece of interference. Sommerville's mother has very firm beliefs about how a child should be reared. 'Leave the disciplining,'" she mimicked in matriarchal tones, "'to those who have made it their business to know the workings of small children,' were her words to Thea when last I visited."

"How unfortunate for Lady Sommerville—"

"My sentiments precisely! How thoroughly we understand each other."

Duncan glanced at her quizzically. "I hesitate to destroy this moment of complete understanding, but I was about to say, 'How unfortunate for Lady Sommerville to be caught between the influences of two exceedingly determined female relations.' She must not know which way to turn."

"Any aid *I* have rendered my sister has been at her request." Alys stopped on the last step, allowing

Duncan to go before her, so that she might have the advantage of an equal height.

"Yes, your sister has a very amiable disposition. Ned has remarked upon this virtue of hers on more than one occasion. I daresay his deep regard for her has kept him from speaking out about the little intrusions that occur when certain guests come to visit."

She glared at him. "Would you care—or dare—to make your meaning more plain, sir?"

"I will only say, before I bid you good-night, that her ladyship finds happiness in making others happy. If one she loves finds happiness in determining the course of others' lives, then she is content to be carried by the, ah, force of the current." He bowed and turned to leave her.

"Are you suggesting," she said, coming after him, "that to make me happy my sister allows me to interfere?"

He silently strolled along the corridor, as if deep in thought, until he paused before a door. "Those are your own words and you must make of them what you will. I'm j'st a lowly north-countryman, unversed in the subtle inferences of Society. Good night, Miss Champion," he murmured, slipping into the chamber and closing the door before she could reply.

"Blast! Subtle inferences? Lowly north-countryman, indeed!" She would show him subtle inferences. She grabbed the latch, quite prepared to continue what had been left unsettled between them.

Just in time she recalled that as an unmarried lady she could hardly enter a gentleman's chamber without forfeiting her reputation. She kicked the door with her sandalled foot, and swiftly discovered the foolishness of the childish act as a sharp pain shot from her toes up her leg.

With as much dignity as she could muster, she hobbled to her allotted bedchamber. Before retiring, she silently set a small stack of coins on the dressing-table for Emma, the winner of their wager. The maid seemed satisfied to give Alys a knowing look as she pocketed her winnings. Then she left her mistress alone with her thoughts.

Alys had gambled on Giles's attentiveness and lost. Since she was neither plain nor disfigured, she believed that her case was not irredeemable. She drifted to sleep with the hope that her infuriating instructor truly could teach her how to catch a man's fancy.

The next day, when she entered the morning-room, Alys found that she would not have the peace of a solitary breakfast even though most of the gentlemen had long since retired to the library. Duncan Todd sat wholly occupied with a sporting journal, the warm glow of sunlight falling upon his head and shoulders. From the window behind him, the woodland scene, which was framed by new spring foliage, seemed quite suited to his attire of breeches and top-boots. Even his loose-fitting coat had a rustic appearance.

He caught her staring at him. Lowering the journal, Duncan slowly smiled, but remained silent.

A little disconcerted, yet determined to gain the upper hand, Alys said, "You, sir, are a most provoking man."

"Am I?" he asked, his tone ingenuous; then he seemed to ponder the possibility. "A lady who's easily excited—one prone to passionate outbursts—would find me so. I daresay you know the sort; she enters a room without offering as much as a 'Good day,' or 'How's the bacon?'"

Alys suppressed her desire to make a passionate response. She would not give him the gratification. How did he do it? How did he manage to turn her words back upon her, making her look slightly ridiculous? She'd never yet encountered a man who could best her, and she determined to expose the faults and foibles of this one.

"Good morning, Mr. Todd," she said with a forced smile. She inclined her head graciously. "Is the bacon edible? Thea's cook is not always at his best in the morning." She moved to the sideboard and lifted the lid of a chafing-dish. "Fish?"

"Carp, the queen of river fish," he replied, folding the journal and setting it aside, "caught early this morning."

The small-mouthed fish seemed to look up at her accusingly. "Did you—"

"Hooked her with a big, fat worm. The proper bait is half the battle. She went happily into the skillet."

Alys swallowed hard, feeling her appetite wane. "It doesn't seem quite fair, luring her to her death with something she cannot resist."

"Life is seldom fair, but there is order in all things. You are desirous of luring a certain gentleman to the death of his bachelorhood. To do so you must use the proper bait." He looked at her critically and came closer to further his examination. "You dress very becomingly. Last night your gown would have caught the eye of a blind man, but our Mr. Pomeroy did not seem to notice." He walked around her, then leant down and sniffed the air about her head. "Fresh. Clean. Just a hint of rose-water." He stepped back and frowned. "It won't do at all."

"What won't do?"

"Your scent. If I remember correctly, from my limited years at the university, the word *allure* means 'to entice by charm or attraction.' An angler attracts his fish by using the proper *lure,* using bait that catches the eye and teases the senses. Some argue that a fish cannot smell—"

"Can it?"

Duncan smiled and shrugged. "I really do not know. But if one believes the fish lore, then yes, it can. And, curiously, the fish will come out when one applies the right scent on the lure." He took her hands in his and stood back, surveying her. "You are a demmed fetching lure, my girl, and we are about to discover the proper scent for you."

She looked at him with a dubious eye. "Have I been using an improper scent?"

"Not improper, but ineffective. Your scent should tease a gentleman's senses until he's drawn to your side. After you've finished your repast, we will begin our quest for that fragrance. Shall I join you in your dressing-room? Perhaps you would wish her ladyship's presence to lend propriety to the occasion."

Alys shook her head. Thea was the last person she wanted to know of such a hare-brained scheme. "My maid will suffice. Shall we meet at the hour?"

He bowed his acquiescence and left her to breakfast in peace. But her hunger had fled along with her peace of mind. She nibbled on toast and sipped tea while she considered her deepening course.

She was more than ever determined to capture Giles's affections. Yet how had control of her venture passed from her hands into those of Duncan Todd? He was an exasperating man, quite unmanageable. And she had the unsettling feeling that he was making sport of her, even though everything he'd said about the importance of the proper bait made good sense.

She resolved that she would assume command of their future dealings. To meet him in her dressing-room would establish her position of authority. Yet the thought of him entering her chamber was disconcerting; no, even more than disconcerting...it was dangerous.

CHAPTER FOUR

"EMMA, WHERE DID YOU get those bottles of scent?"
Alys sat before her dressing-table, waiting and fidgeting with a fan.

Her maid smiled in a secret manner. "Charles, Mr.
Todd's man, brought me a message from his master.
He said I was to borrow as many bottles as her ladyship would lend." She held out the tray she carried.
"This is the lot of them." With an inquisitive sidelong glance, Emma set the tray on the table, then assumed a servile posture. "Will you be needing
anything else, Miss Alys?"

"Just your presence for—" A knock at her chamber door interrupted her. She motioned for Emma to
admit the caller. "Hurry, please. Do not keep Mr.
Todd waiting."

Emma nearly tripped when she wrenched about in
midstride to gape at her mistress. "Mr. Todd is coming in *here?*"

Assuming a commanding attitude, Alys levelled a
cool look at her maid. "If you leave him standing in
the corridor any longer every footman and maid shall
know of his visit. You wretch, let him in!"

Duncan entered as if he were making a social call at a Grosvenor Square drawing-room. There wasn't a hint of furtiveness to his movements or stealth in his step. His demeanour suggested it was quite an ordinary occurrence for him to attend a lady in her chambers.

"La, miss, I never thought to see a gentleman enter your dressing-room," Emma blurted out. She clapped a hand over her mouth, shrugged apologetically, then took her place by her mistress's side.

Groaning inwardly, Alys could feel the situation slipping away from her. With a stiff wave of her hand, she indicated that Duncan should seat himself.

He placed his chair very near her own. "Miss Champion, allow me to correct any misconception your maid might be labouring under." He grinned in a friendly manner at Emma. "I am here as an advisor... as an expert in the use of the lure." He indicated the bottles of scent. "Miss Champion is in need of the proper lure to catch the attention of her swain. Shall we proceed?"

Alys nodded as she vigorously fanned her heated cheeks. She dare not even think what Emma must be imagining. It was all too mortifying.

"To find the proper essence," he continued, addressing himself to Emma, "we must first consider our prey. Mr. Pomeroy has a love of books. His keenest interest is in things of the past. No doubt he would find a musty, earthy scent to his liking." Duncan turned his attention to Alys and scrutinized her through half-closed eyes.

She found her stomach tightening as his regard deepened.

"We must unfold the mysteries that lie hidden beneath Miss Champion's cool façade." Duncan leaned towards her and looked deeply into her eyes.

He was so close that Alys thought for a moment that he would kiss her. She hardly breathed, yet she didn't pull away. She returned his gaze openly, as she took in the blueness of his eyes and the thick, dark fringe that edged them. She tried to remember the colour of Giles's eyes, but that image wouldn't come to mind. The more she looked into Duncan's eyes the more she became lost to everything except his magnetic gaze.

A gusty sigh from Emma broke this spell.

Drawing a ragged breath, Alys found that her palms had become moist and her hands trembled. Was a gentleman supposed to have this sort of effect on a lady?

For a long moment Duncan said nothing. When he spoke, his voice was low and husky, rumbling from the depths of his chest. "There is a spirit about you that is elusive, almost mystical. I've a notion, Miss Champion, that you have too much womanliness for such a one as Mr. Pomeroy. The heat that comes from your inner fires would surely scorch the fingers of a scholar."

Emma sighed loudly.

Alys swallowed hard and tried to compose herself. Never had such words been spoken to her. She found them glorious and frightening. Without warning, her eyes clouded with tears. She'd always wanted Giles to say such things to her. In her scheme, Duncan Todd was not the man she ought to hear them from.

"Forgive me for speaking forthrightly," Duncan said as he eased back from her.

She blinked her tears away. "You were to tell me of allure. The best bait to use, remember?"

"My dear Miss Champion, you have more allure than is respectable. You've just not learned how to draw upon your powers. Now... for bait." He set the tray of bottles on her lap. "I would say an earthy, woody scent with a touch of spice to enhance your mystery. Something warm and vibrant to kindle those hidden fires."

He pulled one stopper after another and sniffed their fragrances. At last he came upon one that caused him to pause. He raised his brow in speculation. "May I?" he asked, taking her by the wrist. He unfastened the tightly fitting sleeve and slowly pushed the fabric up her arm, his fingertips brushing her soft skin like a caress.

Alys felt a warm tingle move gently over her and she nearly drew back from him.

Duncan turned the bottle on end and allowed the perfume to liberally douse his fingertip. Then he took

Alys's arm in a clasp that was far too intimate. He stroked her wrist with a sensuous touch, soft but intense, letting the scent penetrate where it would. The *coup de grâce* came as he lowered his head and blew gently, like a lover's whisper, on her tingling flesh.

Alys's sharp intake of breath was covered by Emma's louder gasp. "La, sir, is your man as handy with the ladies as you?" the maid asked in a faint voice.

Duncan glanced up from his pleasurable task and peered at Alys. "Have I offended you? We north-countrymen don't always observe Society's rules of decorum."

"You northerns," Emma interjected, "know a few niceties that surely tickle a lady's fancy."

As if oblivious to the maid's presence, he kept his gaze fixed upon Alys, mutely holding her captive. He raised her wrist for her judgement. "Is it to your liking, Miss Champion?" His look warmed her. "Does the fragrance please you?"

"I—I—" Alys stuttered, not knowing quite how to reply.

Duncan inhaled the perfume and frowned. "No, I don't think this one fully suits you. That elusive quality is missing."

"I have just the thing." Emma went to the clothes press and searched its depths. She returned cradling a small vial in her hands and proffered it to Duncan.

Taking the small bottle, he looked enquiringly at Alys. "Were you saving this... perhaps for something special?"

She nodded. "My mother mixed the scented oil for me long ago. She said I was to use it for..." A blush rose to her cheeks. Then she raised her head and stared him in the eye. "I was to use it for my marriage night."

With tender reverence, he eased the stopper off and breathed in the fragrance. A slow appreciative smile crept over his face. "Your mother was a woman of insight. It takes a rare talent to produce such a delightful result. Of course, it must be your decision, but would you allow me the liberty?" he asked, holding out his hand for hers.

For a moment she hesitated. The perfume had been meant for the personal pleasure of her husband. Yet, if she didn't use it to lure Giles to her side, how would she ever have a husband? Shyly she undid the fastening of her other sleeve and held out her wrist to him.

This time the application proceeded in a different manner. Duncan's attitude became solemn, touched with a humility that lent an air of ceremony to the anointing.

He allowed time for the oil to penetrate, then with great reverence savoured the essence. Finally he took her hand in his and kissed it. "Miss Champion, I envy the lucky fellow who becomes your husband. It was a master-stroke to add that hint of peaches. All in all, 'tis a marvellous scent. Innocently voluptuous without a touch of unseemliness to it, that's my opinion—should you care to value the judgement of an under-bred north-country farmer.''

"Oh, you've a way with you, sir," Emma uttered, looking as pleased as she could be. "There's some who might choose the opinion of a scholar over that of a manly farmer, but there's no accounting for a female's foibles."

"We must remember that love is blind and some must be led by the hand to true love," he remarked with a surreptitious wink.

Emma chuckled softly.

"Whatever are you two talking about?" Alys asked. "A certain gentleman may be unaware as yet of my womanliness," she said, as she sniffed the scent, "but that unfortunate circumstance is about to be remedied."

"Allow me to assist you, Miss Champion," Duncan said, taking the vial and dabbing scent on his fingertip. He stroked it from behind her ear down the soft column of her neck.

Alys shivered, but permitted him to repeat the slow stroke again from behind her other ear. She managed to ask, "Where did you learn of these things, which concern only females?"

"A true gentleman should be knowledgeable about all things concerning a lady." He gazed at her until a devilish light played in his eyes, easing the moment. "Besides, I've five sisters who have shared many mysteries that are particularly womanish. Forthright to a fault, my sisters are.''

"I have a notion that the dear girls must have disconcerted you many times." She enjoyed the thought of his sisters embarrassing him.

"They did tell me once that the most important place to apply scent is—ah, very near to where one's heart beats. I shall leave you to interpret that as you will." Duncan stood and inhaled. "Wonderful scent. We must hope that Mr. Pomeroy does not bury his nose all day in a book." He turned to Emma. "Be sure your mistress wears her hair in a softer manner than is her usual mode. Last night she had curls dancing about the back of her neck—quite fetching! She must look very approachable, inviting." He breathed in the lingering fragrance on his fingertip and a wistful expression passed over his face. "Remember that the use of the correct bait is half the battle."

"Is this all a lady needs to know of allure?" asked Alys.

"Certainly not. But we mustn't rush our fences. Slow and steady wins the race." He opened the door and peered along the corridor. "Come down to the library as soon as you're ready. A little mild flirtation might pique Mr. Pomeroy's interest."

"You wish me to conduct a dalliance with Mr. Pomeroy?"

He smiled at her as he stepped out into the corridor. "No, with me," he replied, disappearing before she could utter a retort.

"WORDS CANNOT EXPRESS what is in my heart," Giles said to the gentlemen assembled in the library. "To have my own copy of the writings is a dream come true. Now, while some of us dallied the morning away—" he glared at Duncan "—those of us who are truly devoted to the study of the ancients were labouring hard in our preparations for the rubbings. We are about to proceed to the step that requires particular care. There is an art to making rubbings. Signore Senusi, you no doubt have supervised many such procedures before in the course of your studies. Would you care to take charge?"

Senusi's eyes widened momentarily. "I would not rob you of the honour, Mr. Pomeroy. And, as you must know, the European way of doing things is much different from the English. I have come to your country to be the student, not the master. It is I who sits at your feet to learn. As a scholar, your repute reaches beyond the shores of your island."

"You flatter me." Giles's cheeks reddened as he smoothed back his flowing hair. Yet his stance became more authoritative and his bearing waxed lofty.

Duncan leaned back against a work-table and shook his head slowly. *What the deuce does she find agreeable in this jackanapes?* he wondered. Could it be that

Pomeroy was the sort that could be easily managed? Or was it his elusiveness to matrimony that made her so determined to have him? Some wise old Roman once opined that "We desire nothing so much as what we ought not to have." Was it so with Alys?

"Mr. Todd, you do not appear to be heeding what I have been saying. I daresay your interest in the Stone is lukewarm." Giles put his hand on the black slab of rock as if to shield it from the indifference of the ignorant. His stance became even more protective when someone tapped on the library door.

Alys entered, bringing with her Lady Sommerville.

"My interest grows by the minute, Mr. Pomeroy," Duncan remarked as he nodded a greeting to the ladies. He noticed that instead of the knot at the nape of her neck, Alys now wore her lovely blond hair in loose curls caught up by a ribbon.

Sommerville ushered his wife to a chair and fussed over her. "Why did you come down without the aid of your sedan-chair? You mustn't strain yourself. Dr. Wingate—"

"Is a fusty old woman. Dr. Knighton, a well-respected accoucheur, says that exercise is beneficial. Doesn't he, Alys?"

Alys turned from gazing at Giles and looked enquiringly at her sister.

"Dearest Alys," Thea said, "you must tell Sommerville about Dr. Knighton's opinions. I know that I should blush to repeat them. Or perhaps this isn't the place for such talk.''

Giles groaned and drew protectively closer to the Stone.

Seeming to sense the unrest building in the scholar, Alys quickly promised Sommerville a private interview later, then turned her attention to Giles and the Stone. Senusi, who'd claimed his place next to her as soon as she'd entered, never left her side as she glided from one group to another.

''Such a wonderful piece of antiquity,'' Alys said, stepping close to Giles. ''It must be shared with the world.'' She made a grand gesture, waving her arm under his nose.

Ah, Duncan thought as he watched her manoeuvre, the scent, of course. Perhaps he should have offered her a few words about subtlety. He smiled to himself. He wasn't that great a fool. However, it galled him to know that the special perfume was being enjoyed by that intellectual lout.

Pomeroy sneezed. ''What is that odd odour in the air?''

''A divine aroma,'' Senusi exclaimed rapturously.

Lifting his shoes one at a time, Giles eyed the bottom of each with suspicion. ''Perchance while on my morning stroll I stepped where I should not have.''

Duncan bit back a laugh. Apparently, Mr. Pomeroy suffered a defect in his sense of smell.

With a look of deep chagrin and mortification, Alys eased away from Giles. "Old things oft-times have an unsavory odour."

"Do you refer to the Stone, Miss Champion?" Giles asked in an incredulous tone. "She is everything that is pure and rare."

"Which is why the Stone should be shared," she replied. "Viewed by everyone ... even young children."

"Children?" Giles seemed clearly apprehensive.

"Alys, you dear girl!" Thea exclaimed. "Are the children coming down?"

Smiling confidently, Alys announced, "Nanny Jinks is bringing the girls down on an expedition of an edifying nature. They are to view the Stone and listen to Mr. Pomeroy explain about it."

"Little girls in a library?" Giles uttered in a faint voice, combing back his hair with a trembling hand.

Sommerville appeared pleased. "I cannot remember when that officious nanny last allowed the girls down among company. However did you persuade her, Alys? What sort of wonder-working did you perform?"

"Never ask to look up the sleeve of a conjurer. Merely sit back and enjoy the magic of the moment." Alys paused to listen and turned towards the door. With a wave of her hand, she said, "Hocus-pocus!"

Into the room came a blond-haired young miss of about ten years followed by a timid younger sister who favoured her father with her serious demeanour and brown hair. Nelly entered last under the restraining hand of Nanny Jinks. Even when the little three-year-old tripped on the carpet she didn't fall, for the nanny's grip was quite firm.

"Mama!" Nelly cried as she caught sight of her mother. The invitation of her mother's open arms was all the little girl needed to give her strength to break from the nanny's clutches.

"Now, my dear girl," Sommerville said as his youngest daughter tumbled into his wife's arms, "go gently. The doctor doesn't want your mama having too much excitement."

Nelly went from her mother and embraced Sommerville about his legs, giving him an exuberant squeeze. "Papa, I missed you. You must come to see me every day."

"His lordship is a very busy man," Nanny Jinks stated in lofty tones, holding her angular body exaggeratedly erect. "He is occupied with many very important matters. And it is very naughty of you, Miss Eleanor, to speak so boldly to your father—very naughty indeed."

"I daresay she's merely excited to be visiting her parents," Alys said.

The nanny clasped her hands together. "I strive *very* diligently to instill in my charges a *very* strong sense of decorum." She snapped her fingers when she spied the oldest girl sidling towards her mother. "Miss Elizabeth, you may wait while your younger sister, Miss Gabriella, pays her tribute to her ladyship.''

"Nanny Jinks," Alys said, guiding the woman away from the family circle, "I think you might be *very* comfortable sitting here by the window. The warm sunlight will do you good—put some colour in your cheeks.''

"I *very* much fear," the nanny said, rubbing her flat chest, "that I've contracted a chill. My charges make a habit of slipping outdoors and involving themselves in all sorts of mischief. Miss Elizabeth is far too adventuresome for her own good and likes nothing better than to lead her younger sisters astray." Her face pulled into a puckering scowl. "The schoolroom is the proper place for young girls.''

Alys grinned amiably. "How wise you are, to be sure. And this short time of enrichment will no doubt benefit the Misses Pomeroy. Rest easy now." She left the nanny and moved to join the others, but was waylaid.

With a dubious frown, Duncan watched Senusi ingratiate himself with her and attempt to instigate a flirtation. He decided to give the foreigner just enough time in her company so that Alys would welcome an interruption.

"Mademoiselle—I—I mean," Senusi said, faltering, "*Signorina* Champion, you brought with you the brightness of the spring sunlight when you entered this dull and gloomy chamber. And how good to see her ladyship and her little girls join us. No doubt we can credit you with this double pleasure. You are a lady of great resourcefulness." He looked at her with longing. "A man could lose himself in the delight of unveiling the solution of the mystery which lies hidden within your soul. Ah, I have stepped beyond the—how do you say it?—the mark. But you see before you a man whose fires match the great heat of his country."

"I had not thought Italy was so very hot," she said, looking perplexed.

Senusi cleared his throat and pulled on his collar. "I was speaking of *southern* Italy."

"Have you left your country because of the war?"

"Signore Senusi," Giles called, "are you ready to proceed?"

"The war?" Senusi ignored Giles. His complete attention remained focused on Alys. "Ah, yes—I mean, *si, signorina.* When the conqueror Napoleon came to our country he tried to change everything. That which he took from our country we want back." He glanced from the Stone to his manservant, who remained silent but watchful from his place by the wall. "I am tempted to follow the Frenchman's example and take with me from England something of value—a sample of its natural beauty. Have you ever seen the waters of the Mediterranean Sea? One day I would like to show them to you."

"*Signore?*" Giles queried in an exasperated tone. "You, little girl, don't touch that." He picked up Nelly and set her away from the Stone. "Miss Champion, could you do something with this child?"

Alys left Senusi without a word and took Nelly by the hand. She glanced beseechingly at Duncan.

"Young ladies," Duncan said, bowing in a courtly manner, "please be seated and prepare to be edified by Mr. Pomeroy."

Nelly looked ready to cry. "Is that man going to eat me?" she asked, apparently confused by the word *edified*.

"No," Duncan replied in a low voice. "He's going to teach you."

Nelly's expression didn't change. She slowly seated herself on the sofa between her two sisters. "Betsy," she whispered to her oldest sibling, "does he use a switch like Nanny Jinks?"

"Please proceed, Mr. Pomeroy," Alys said with a determined smile. "We are all eager to hear what you have to say about the Stone."

"Very good," Duncan whispered to her. "Showing an interest in a man's occupation is always a clever stratagem."

Giles took a protective position before the Rosetta Stone. "This is a very rare and important relic of ancient Egypt. It was discovered in the small village of Rashid by the French in the year 1799. There are three different forms of text on it."

Nelly yawned.

"In April of 1802," Giles continued in a monotone voice, "nearly ten years ago, the Reverend Stephen Weston read the first English translation of the Greek text to the Society of Antiquaries in London. Those of us who have a deep love and devotion for the Rosetta Stone have continued the work of deciphering the remaining texts. Today, we are making ink rubbings."

"Can we help?" Nelly asked, hopping down from her perch.

"Certainly not!" Giles looked horrified at the notion. "Miss Champion, would you take Miss Eleanor in hand?"

Lord Sommerville left his wife's side and advanced upon the little group gathered about the Stone. "It would be instructive to explain the procedure. Humour me in this, if you please, Giles."

The scholar again took up his lecturing stance. Grudgingly he began his explanation. When he came to the use of the ink the other two girls slipped off the sofa and inched their way forward. Their curiosity drew them nearer to the work-table.

Standing on tiptoe, Nelly tried to see what her sisters were looking at. In her determination to give herself a boost she set her hand in a large bowl of ink.

Giles gasped and rushed forward. He collided with Nelly as she swung round to see what was amiss. Her tiny handprint stained Mr. Pomeroy's sleeve. As he flung her hand away from him, a sprinkling of ink arched over Nelly's sisters.

Amid the girlish shrieks, the nanny's shrill scolding, the scholar's outraged bellow, the library door opened and a footman announced, "Miss Henrietta Champion." At the prodding of a cane, the footman added, "And Master McVicar." A tiny white-haired woman, no bigger than a young girl, entered with a Skye terrier at her side.

She seemed satisfied with the state of turmoil in the room. "There's nothing like a warm welcome to make an old woman feel wanted. Master McVicar, go and pay your respects to the little girls." The dog entered into the confusion with several exuberant barks. "Thea, how well you look. Where's the baby?"

"The baby?" her ladyship repeated in a faint voice. "Sommerville, tell Giles to cease his shouting."

Alys stepped in and began to settle everyone down. Mr. Pomeroy, however, was in a high temper. He retreated to the Stone, muttering strong words to himself.

"Great-Aunt Etta," Alys said, "naturally Thea welcomes you any time you care to visit, but she has not yet delivered her babe. Nanny Jinks, take the girls back upstairs, and there is to be no punishment—no back-boards. Nelly's mishap was unintentional." She didn't seem to hear Giles's loud growling response. "I daresay we could all use a quiet moment. Sommerville, would you see Thea to her rooms? And Aunt Etta, perhaps after you have rested we ladies could gather in Thea's chamber to have a nice long chat. Mr. Todd, would you lend my great-aunt your escort?''

One by one Alys emptied the library, until just she and Giles remained. Duncan wondered what she would say to him and wanted very much to be privy to whatever transpired, but the little woman by his side appeared intent upon his attendance. Henrietta Champion handed him her dog, cautioning him not to hold the terrier too tightly.

''He has an unsavoury malady, don't you know,'' Aunt Etta remarked, wrinkling her nose.

Sommerville, following behind with his wife, leant forward and whispered, ''We are never sure if it's the dog or Aunt Etta who suffers from the . . . the unfortunate spells.''

Warned just in time, Duncan tried to ignore the very foul odour which soon permeated the air. Aunt Etta paused on the stairs to withdraw from her reticule a small oval-shaped device which was attached to a chain. Smiling, she swung it to and fro. The smell of rotten eggs was quickly masked by the strong scent of jasmine.

With eyes watering, Duncan recalled the very intoxicating perfume that Alys wore and sighed wistfully. He wondered if she would be able to bring the scholar to heel. He hoped not.

CHAPTER FIVE

"MISS CHAMPION, never have I witnessed such a display of unruliness!" Giles glanced down at the damp ink print on his sleeve. "Those young girls should never have been allowed within the hallowed walls of this library. A library is a place of quiet and studious labours. It is not the place for such distractions as children and ladies."

Alys had been meekly taking the full force of his outburst, but she raised her head at this last remark. She opened her mouth, ready to make a rebuttal, but he continued without a pause.

"It was all your doing, Miss Champion. You violated the sanctity of this library by bringing her ladyship down—going against the orders of her knowledgeable physician—to visit his lordship, who was occupied with matters of great moment. Then—then..." He raked a hand through his long hair and closed his eyes as if in pain. "Then you had the idiotic idea of introducing a gaggle of little girls into this sacred chamber. What was it you called it? Ah, yes—an expedition of an edifying nature. Allow me to say that the nature of—of those young hoydens was very encroaching. Why were they not left in the nursery where they belong?''

''I—''

''Yes, you had some ridiculous notion and, being a female, you could not but follow your inclination. I had thought better of you, Miss Champion.''

She looked up hopefully. ''You did? What did you think of me, Mr. Pomeroy?''

''Why... that you were a level-headed female... who, as a spinster, knew her place in the society of her family.''

Her own temper took a sudden leap. *Knew her place, indeed!* She was about to make a scathing retort, but he turned away and went to his precious stone. He stroked it lovingly. Why had he never touched her like that? Duncan Todd's fiery caress came to mind and she shivered. If she ever wanted Giles to stroke her in such a way she would have to humble herself and make amends to him. She forced herself not to think of the toll it would cost her to grovel. She supposed she would have to pay the price, for, after all, her good intentions and scheming lay at the root of the entire sorry episode.

Her first venture at allurement had gone awry.

Quite unbidden, thoughts came to her of the way Duncan Todd had looked into her eyes. He'd seen within her the most marvellous things. Why did Giles never look directly into her eyes? Would he see as much as the north-country farmer had? She had to know the answer. "Mr. Pomeroy, would you look into my eyes?" she asked, coming up beside him.

He turned to her with a frown. "Is something amiss with them?"

"I hope you'll find something."

"Have you a cinder troubling you? Here, let me look." He peered at her, squinting. "I see nothing."

"Nothing? Please, look closer."

He stepped back from her. "I think such an intimate sort of inspection should be performed by your maid, Miss Champion. If you'll excuse me, I must change my ruined coat." He began to leave her, but turned about. "I hope you did not take my chastisement as a personal reproof. I am fully aware that the female judgement often errs." He smiled in an abstracted manner. "Actually, Miss Champion, you are one of the finest females of my acquaintance, and usually very sensible. I cannot understand why you've never married." He shrugged and departed, leaving her with her mouth agape.

In another part of the house, in one of the smaller chambers, another pair also held a private conversation. Fearful of the servants, the conspirators kept their voices low as they spoke in their native tongue.

"Noble Baka, you must be patient," Senusi said. "It is written, 'Act with caution and you shall undoubtedly triumph over a powerful enemy.' We must wait and plan. Watch for our moment."

Baka glared at him and folded his arms over his chest. "You do too much watching. But it is women you watch. As your commander, I order you to cease your idle ways. You will read the Roll of Fate once more and, for your sake, I pray that we are bidden to take action."

With a look of incredulity, Senusi said, "Most Noble of the Noble, you misjudge me. If you doubt my honest readings, then take the roll yourself."

"You know full well that I cannot read it. But I have eyes to see. I have watched you lust for the unmarried fair one. You are a fool. She is old." Baka pulled his coat closer. "I grow weary of this cold country. We must quickly obey Kamose's orders, then we can return to our own land, where the sun never hides itself."

"Your longing for home has clouded your eyes. If we try to take the Stone and fail, these people will place guards all around it, then we shall surely never bring it back to Egypt. We must have a plan. Besides, a man is warm enough if he wears *all* of his clothes." Senusi enjoyed his elegant European garments. But he particularly liked the diaphanous coverings favoured by the ladies.

Baka scowled and muttered to himself, "It goes against nature to girdle a man in such a way."

Looking down at his pantaloons, Senusi admired the close fit of the cloth and the pleasing aspect of his well-formed leg. The only impediment was that it took so long to remove them, and passion often flared with a speed faster than the nimblest of fingers. "We must dress in the manner of the English. Remember Kamose's words to us, 'Be like the Nile while in that strange land. The Nile is silent, seeming to have no certain current.' We would not be silent if we went about in our robes. We must continue to fool these people."

"The tall one watches us. He is not so easily fooled."

"Does the Noble Baka fear him? You need not. As long as the scholar is our friend we will have no trouble from the large farmer." Senusi's brow furrowed and he was thoughtful. "But he is not at all like any farmer I have ever seen. These English are a strange people."

"They are too pale."

Senusi considered one white and delightsome female to be very much to his liking. "We must linger as long as is needful. It is written on the Roll of Fate that 'If you are discreet, you shall gain the object on which your heart is fixed.' We shall yet gain our reward. For 'Fortune favours the brave and enterprising.'" He enjoyed using the Roll of Fate to his advantage. Holding control over his leader, the Noble Baka, gave him great satisfaction. "Our destiny is in the hands of Fate," he said with a knowing smile.

ALYS LEANED on the terrace rail. Surely, she thought, Providence would favour the worthy endeavours of an upright spinster. Wasn't she deserving of a husband? What great wrong could she have done to warrant her continued solitary state? After a brief review, she could find no serious transgression which needed addressing.

Perhaps she wasn't at fault. Perhaps Duncan Todd had been correct when he said that she didn't lack allure, but just lacked the knowledge of how to draw upon it.

She held up her wrist and breathed in the lingering fragrance. Sighing wistfully, she thought how Giles would never savour its essence. She tried to envision their wedding day, but the image seemed to evade her. Without the special scent her dream was incomplete.

Upon reflection she knew that she had attempted to undertake too much at one time. From that moment forward she would have to take the courting of Giles in easy stages. Trying to foist the girls on him just to see how he fared with children had been a serious mistake. She should have arranged for the girls to visit Thea privately.

Next time . . . next time would be different. She was determined that it would be so.

"Wool-gathering or day-dreaming?"

She frowned at Duncan. "We ladies prefer to say that we are pausing for a moment of quiet reflection." Turning from him, she gazed up at the sky.

"My sisters used to pine in the same manner when the desire of their heart was just out of their reach. But as I recall they ceased to behave like moonlings after the first flush of youth passed."

"Are you implying that I am acting like a young girl fresh from the schoolroom?" She glared at him.

Duncan rubbed his chin and smiled sheepishly. "If I said anything so feather-brained you'd box my ears...and you'd have a right to such action. But I've noticed that you have made a habit of attaching a meaning to my words which extends far beyond my intent."

"I daresay I *had* attached greater meaning to your words when you said that I possessed more allure than was respectable. Mr. Pomeroy was nearly repelled!"

"Ah yes, but Signore Senusi was captivated."

She exhaled heavily, not bothering to hide the impatience that his suggestion engendered. "He is a guest of my brother-in-law's and I could not snub him. But why was he so attentive and Giles so...so circumspect?"

"Miss Champion, I am *shocked* that you would insinuate such a dreadful thing about our poor Mr. Pomeroy."

"What did I insinuate?" she asked, looking genuinely perplexed.

"My dear girl, your indelicacy has unmanned me. And 'tis demmed imprudent of you to make an assumption about the scholar without a great preponderance of evidence." He appeared to struggle for words.

"Would you speak plainly, sir?"

"There are certain things ladies and gentlemen never mention. But I must dispel your erroneous notion." He stepped back from her, as if wanting to disassociate himself, and gazed off at the river.

Alys stared at him.

"I shall make this observation," he said, "then we must never speak of it again." He looked at her squarely. "A woman should not assume merely on the evidence of a man ignoring her that he has a liking for his own kind."

She gripped the terrace railing and stared out at the surrounding park.

"And as for Mr. Pomeroy's obvious loathing of children," he said after a lengthy pause, "a scholar cannot be expected to tolerate the noisy chatterings of young girls. Can we ask a scholar to share the attitudes of a normal man? The importance of his work must be considered. Should a man sacrifice it for life with a family?"

Her thoughts she kept to herself.

"After all," Duncan continued relentlessly, "the man's work *is* his life and love. All his passion is given to those objects from long, long ago. His concerns for the present do not exist. The woman who adores him will have to accept his neglect and the demands of his studies, for they benefit the world, do they not? Surely you wouldn't wish him to give up everything for your happiness?''

She moved along the terrace away from him. ''Is it unreasonable for a lady to expect a gentleman to share his existence in the prescribed manner, sanctioned by Divine Law...and the laws of King and Country? Could not a woman give courage to the man in his struggles? Could not a woman give aid, bringing order to his existence? She could help him achieve his goal, could she not?'' She whirled about and faced him. ''My opinion of Mr. Pomeroy is quite different from yours. A sporting gentleman could hardly be expected to understand a scholar. Men made for sports are only interested in the chase. They live for the moment of capture. Mr. Pomeroy isn't like my father, who was too concerned with himself to be aware of the needs of others.''

''Were my mother here to advise you, she would say beware, lest you lose the substance by grasping the shadow. Are you quite sure of your man?''

''Quite sure. All he lacks is the proper opportunity to bring forth his fine qualities. At the moment he is very much occupied with the Stone.'' She cast him a challenging glance, daring him to dispute her.

Quietly he returned her look, then said, ''Yes, very occupied. How fortunate it is that you share all his interests. He'll count himself lucky indeed when you've captured his fancy. He will no doubt praise your tenacity and your determination in the quest.

Nothing flatters a man more than to know he is wanted. I bow to your superior knowledge of the gentleman.''

She inclined her head in return.

''Will you still be needing the guidance of an expert sporting man?'' he enquired politely.

With less bravado, she thought of her first foray into her own particular field of the hunt. She knew she had to take whatever advice she was offered in order to bring Giles out from cover and give him chase. Though lacking a complete degree of confidence, she raised her head proudly and said, ''It behooves me to use all the advantages at hand.'' She paused thoughtfully. ''Mr. Pomeroy seemed annoyed when Signore Senusi flirted with me. It merely interrupted his work. But for some reason Mr. Pomeroy views you in a different light. Perhaps . . . if you were to show a keen interest in me he would be shaken from his lethargy. Then perhaps he would... Oh, if only the Stone could vanish for just a little while.''

''Do you think the Stone keeps him from noticing you? How well do you know the man you've set your heart on?'' he asked in a sharp tone.

''We have been acquainted for many years. Even a north-countryman must know that ladies and gentlemen are not permitted a close knowledge of each other until a formal announcement is made.''

He shook his head and let out an exasperated rush of air. ''Now, let me think, what were those sterling qualities that allowed our scholar to win your devotion? Was it his meticulous manner of dress that caught your notice? No doubt his eager attentions have won your favour? I daresay you fancied his wit and his turn of phrase?"

"A man who has very little to say when he is in the presence of learned men should not criticize others for their conversation."

"Miss, you are a sharp-tongued vixen when cornered." Duncan seemed to mock himself. "I mistakenly thought you disliked blood sports." Something in his eyes revealed that her attack had left him wounded. "I have always been a wee bit shy in company," he stated, with a touch of regret in his tone.

She looked down, feeling quite ashamed of herself. "It was unforgivable of me to abuse you thusly." She sensed that he would not hold a grudge, and she smiled her relief. "I daresay if you knew Mr. Pomeroy as I do you would not think to turn me from my course." At his soft, scoffing chuckle she folded her arms and glared at him. "I'll have you know, sir, that Mr. Pomeroy possesses a superior mind. His strong sense of propriety has given order to his life. His knowledgeable opinions are respected by the highest in the land. The Prince Regent often seeks his advice. And his thoughtful expression gives one the feeling that no matter the problem, he will solve it." She finished her list with a speed which suggested she had committed it to memory, then flashed Duncan a smirk of satisfaction.

He bowed. ''I surrender to your evident knowledge of the gentleman. Who am I to quibble with a lady whose heart is set on having a rather crusty scholar— a man so thoroughly devoted to antiquities that he cannot see what is before him? I'll not argue with the wisdom of a woman in love. No, not I! I shall merely be at hand should you need my services.'' He bowed again, then turned and left her.

Alys slumped against the railing. He had surrendered to her wishes, yet why did she feel defeated?

Giles was her ideal, she told herself firmly. Their union would bring to her the happiness for which she'd always longed. In him she saw all that would enrich and give greater meaning to her life.

He needed her. She could help him in so many ways. His repute would flourish were she to set her hand to building him up and gaining for him the recognition he deserved.

Besides, Giles had held a place within her heart for so many years that it was unthinkable to imagine she'd erred in her judgement of him. No, he was perfect for her.

She reminded herself that she must consider that Giles was at present more than usually occupied with his endeavours. She must forgive his neglect, for he was truly not himself. His mind was fully occupied with the Stone and there was no room left for thoughts of her.

With a good measure of forbearance, she even exculpated him of the ill-considered remarks he had made when he was scolding her earlier. Giles surely would not have said such things if he knew her better; he only needed a little time and a little more encouragement. She vowed to redouble her efforts to gain his notice and then woo him.

Unfortunately, Giles seemed unwilling to fall in with her plans. He took refuge in the library, not coming out all afternoon. When she did catch a glimpse of him she made sure that she appeared contrite but friendly. He acknowledged her presence in a vague way before turning his attention back to the Stone.

Alys tried not to show her disappointment. She even managed to conceal her frustration when she took tea with her great-aunt and Thea.

However, Aunt Etta made an innocent remark, and with it came the birth of Alys's disquiet.

"Who is that curious young hermit in the library?" the old woman wondered aloud. "Not a member of our family, is he? Couldn't be. None of the Champions have ever had their attics to let. The poor lad is all about in the head. Chased McVicar round and round when he found him sniffing at that ugly, big rock."

"It is an antiquity," Alys interjected.

"So am I, but no one hovers about me with such keen interest. That poor young man is obsessed. Must have windmills in his head." Aunt Etta wrinkled her nose. "McVicar, have you no manners? The mere mention of wind and you..." She pulled out her aromatic device and waved it over the terrier.

Thea smiled at Alys before hiding behind her handkerchief. Alys, however, frowned as she wondered if Giles truly was obsessed with the Stone. Of course not, she chastened herself; as a scholar he had to be devoted to his studies. Yet the beginnings of a doubt lingered; who would have greater importance in Giles's eyes: his wife or a stone?

"Thea, my dear child," said Aunt Etta, "I know I don't stay abreast of what's fashionable, but is it all the crack to have a rock in one's house? Where can I get one for Master McVicar? He has his heart set on having his own."

"I'll have Thea's gardener look for one," Alys offered absently. For the remainder of the afternoon she was pensive and unusually quiet.

Her thoughts gave her no rest, and that night while the household slept soundly Alys had a series of dreams which left her disturbed. The last image she could recollect was the sight of Duncan Todd coming out of the mist on the back of a black charger. As he approached her, he held out his hand as if he wanted her to join him. But when she drew closer she could see the blood of the hunt on his gloved hand.

She woke with a start, her heart pounding. After such a troubled dream, she remained wide awake until a grey morning greeted her.

It rained all that day and most of the next. So bleak was the aspect of the sky that it left the residents of Green Hill House suffering from a mutual affliction of the doldrums. Nanny Jinks suffered the most by succumbing to what Dr. Wingate asserted was the grippe.

Giles was the only one who seemed to enjoy the continuous drizzle. Being shut in suited him quite well. He remained happily occupied with making his rubbings of the Stone.

His seclusion in the library successfully checked Alys's plans for snaring his attention. She wished that something would occur to shake him from his roost, but another evening passed without his company.

Her worrisome dreams continued. During the early hours of the morning, while she was in that state between sleep and waking, a man's bellow rumbled through the house. At first she wasn't sure the sound was real. Then it occurred again, even louder. She fumbled for her wrapper and stumbled from her chamber.

Out in the corridor Giles stood, wearing a dressing-gown that looked as if he'd had it since he first went away to university. Was this what he would look like on their wedding night?

His expression was a mixture of repulsion and hor-ror. In his hand, outstretched before him, he held a large toad by one of its legs.

"I've been defiled!" he wailed.

CHAPTER SIX

DUNCAN CAME OUT of his bedchamber rubbing the sleep from his eyes. He stood for a moment, trying to assess what was afoot.

Giles, his spindly legs protruding from a shabby dressing-gown which was several inches too short, threw a toad onto the floor, then shrieked when it hopped back in his direction. Alys, her hair dishevelled and her bed cap hanging about her shoulders, tried to catch the amphibian, but could not seem to quite bring herself to pick up the warty beast. Thinking only to still the commotion, Duncan went to her aid and captured the toad, then dropped it into the nearest vase.

"That horrid thing was in my chamber pot," Giles exclaimed. "How it got there is beyond—"

"The question is not how it got there, but rather who put it there," Duncan remarked. He then heard the soft scamper of feet on the stairs leading up to the schoolroom. "I would venture to suggest that it was a youthful prank. Tomorrow, or rather today, is April Noddy Day, which explains much."

"April what?" Giles asked with a decided snap of impatience in his voice.

Duncan smiled good-naturedly. "In the north-country we know it as April Noddy Day, but in these parts I daresay you call it April Fools' Day. 'Tis one and the same."

"What has April the first to do with a toad in . . . in my chamber?" Giles ran a hand through his hair, making it stand on end.

Alys looked quite uncomfortable. She pulled on one of the strings of her cap, further upsetting its precarious hold. The cap came completely off, baring the glory of her golden head. She shoved her hair back. "I am afraid that Nanny Jinks has the grippe and the young maid who attends the schoolroom is presently in charge of the girls. Betsy, my eldest niece, is quite brave and will venture anything . . . even capturing toads for a bit of sport."

With an expression of long-suffering, Giles closed his eyes and groaned. "Have those girls no respect, no sense of what is delicate? After working for many, many hours, I returned to my room to retire for the night and what do I find? My peace has been all cut up. I shall not sleep now—not a wink. My important work shall also be a victim of their tomfoolery." He glanced at Alys and appeared to notice the state of her uncovered head. "Of course, if an example of modesty and circumspection were given them, no doubt those young girls would conform to the proper dictums which govern good behaviour. A child is only as good as its keeper. Good night, all!'' He made a dignified retreat into his small chamber and slammed the door after him.

Alys looked down at the cap dangling from her fingers. ''I daresay he was speaking to me. I shall have to take the girls in hand until their nursemaid is quite well.'' She smoothed back her blond hair and tried to put the cap on again. ''I have never considered myself immodest or lacking in refinement. Yet if he thinks I am, then perhaps I should strive to be more prudent.'' She adjusted the cap. ''Is it on straight?''

''Allow me,'' Duncan said, drawing the square of lace-edged linen from her head. He stroked the silken strands of her hair back from her face. Bending down to be at eye-level with the top of her head, he gauged just where the cap should go and placed it there. After a slight adjustment, he tied the ribbons beneath her right ear. He tried to restrain himself, but couldn't resist chucking her gently on the chin. ''You look very fetching, still soft with sleep.''

She moved back from him. ''I hate to doubt a gentleman's word, yet I must, since I've been having the most wretched night's sleep. I daresay I must look quite a fright.''

''Now you mustn't think that it was you who gave our scholar a turn. All the credit, or, ah, blame must go to the toad and his patronesses, the three Misses Pomeroy.''

A shout of anger came from behind the door of Giles's chamber followed by, "Those blasted imps!"

Alys winced, then with a weary sigh stepped bravely toward Giles's door.

"Hold fast there, my girl. You mustn't take the full force of his anger. Let me be of service before he wakes the whole house with his uproar. We mustn't let him disturb her ladyship, who needs her rest more than any of us." Duncan moved Alys aside and bade her retire. Though she cast him a doubtful glance she did as he asked her.

Without troubling to knock or announce himself, Duncan entered the scholar's bedchamber. If necessary he was prepared to use his fist to quiet the fellow.

But before he could raise his hand or his voice an acrid smell assaulted him. "What is that feculent odour?"

Giles sat on the edge of his bed, wiping his eyes. "Horse manure. Those horrid imps have put it in with my coal." He pulled the front of his dressing-gown over his nose. "I unknowingly added the foul stuff to my fire."

While the scholar sat on his bed bemoaning his miserable state, Duncan went round the room pulling back the drapes and opening the windows. He then tended to the fuel on the fire.

Soon the air began to clear. Kneeling before the grate, Duncan sat back on his heels and marvelled that

Giles had not noticed the unusual lumps in his coal bucket.

"I have the headache," Giles said plaintively. "I shall inform his lordship of this most grievous offence. Those children deserve the worst of punishments—a thorough birching!"

Without a word, Duncan helped him into bed. Giles, however, seemed unable to slide all the way down under the sheets. The laughter that Duncan had been restraining since first seeing the scholar with the toad, burst out in deep rolling chuckles.

"Mr. Pomeroy, you've been short-sheeted." Duncan turned away, completely undone by the incredulous look on the fellow's face. It was well worth the silver crown he'd slipped to the abigail Emma, who was full of pluck.

"Those blasted brats!"

Overcoming his mirth, Duncan proceeded to examine the crisp folds of the sheets. "This bed-making was not fashioned by the hand of a child. It would seem that there are several who take you for a fool."

Turning his shoulder on Duncan, as if to ignore him and his words, Giles pushed farther down into the bed. The sound of rending linen stilled his efforts. "In this house a man is not valued for his true worth. I will not have my work interrupted by these trifling slights. I am a man with a purpose. Nothing shall stay my progress. No childish prank shall trouble my mind...at least not for very long. Good night, sir!"

But the next morning, when the gentlemen entered the library to begin their work anew, Giles suffered such a shock that Lord Sommerville had to call for the hartshorn to revive him. The rubbings of the Stone were missing. They'd vanished as if they had never existed.

In a rather abstracted manner, Giles related that he was quite sure he had placed the rubbings in a drawer the night before and had locked the chest that housed them.

Duncan quietly observed the pair of foreigners, who seemed to show no surprise at the disappearance. The manservant Baka kept his eyes lowered, but his shoulders had a proud set to them, as if a desired feat had been achieved. Senusi began to prattle nervously about nothing of importance. Was he afraid of saying too much?

But when Duncan tried to pursue his suspicions, Giles revived himself sufficiently to accuse him of being part of a wicked conspiracy. "I venture to say," uttered the scholar, "and do so without risk of being found in error, that you are the one behind all these vicious attempts to thwart my work. Are you in league with a rival group? Has de Sacy, that French orientalist, a hand in this collusion?"

Shoving the hartshorn nearly up Giles's nose, Sommerville left his cousin and drew Duncan aside. They conversed privately for a few moments. Sommerville cast a murderous glance at Giles, but made a gesture of resignation. Duncan offered a solution which he hoped would satisfy all concerned. With a solemn bow, he withdrew from the library.

LATE IN THE AFTERNOON, Alys paused outside the door of the schoolroom. She leant her head against the doorpost, tired from too many sleepless nights and from the demands of a restive sister who was unusually cross. Through the door she heard the sounds of girlish laughter, and a smile lightened her face. But when the laughter was followed by the deep-timbred tones of a man, her smile dropped into a frown. *A man in the schoolroom?*

Passing over the threshold, Alys stopped short at the sight of Duncan on all fours, followed by Nelly, who tried to assume the same doglike posture but somehow couldn't seem to keep her little posterior from bobbing up in the air. The two were following a trail of torn bits of paper. At the closing of the door, which caused the paper scraps to flutter, Duncan raised his head and smiled.

Nelly cautioned her aunt to be quiet with a finger pressed to her lips. "We're hunting the hares," she whispered.

"Oh, are you?" Alys remarked, a puzzled expression still marring her brow. "Where is my maid, Emma? She was to stay with the girls while I attended to my sister's needs."

"I released Emma from her duty," Duncan said, "when I came up to visit the lasses. She's fetchin' their victuals." He then dropped his voice to a whisper and said, "We are playing Hare and Hounds." As he got to his feet, his smile broadened into a boyish grin. "Did your father never play it with you on brisk wintery days?"

"He was always out hunting the hares himself."

"Whist now, you must learn to forgive him, for he can no longer crave your pardon himself. 'Tis grievous to carry a grudge beyond the grave. Let ye forget and forgive injuries."

She gazed at him for a time, then asked, "Why do you interest yourself in my attitude about my father? Because he was a sportsman?"

"Because he was your father. The poor fellow was probably just shy. Dealing with females may have been the only thing he feared in life."

With marked scepticism, Alys considered his words, then opened her mouth, ready to refute his theory.

"Shh!" Nelly whispered loudly. "You'll scare off the hares—Betsy and Gaby. They're hiding. I will follow their...their scent, and I will find them." She put her nose down to the trail of paper scraps and once again proceeded to follow them.

The giggles coming from behind the door of the connecting bedchamber failed to turn Nelly from her course of action. She doggedly followed the trail. "Come on, Uncle Duncan," she called.

Duncan shrugged at Alys's startled look, then directed Nelly to continue without him. "'Uncle' to Nelly is an innocent title of affection. The girls have begun to think of me as kin," he murmured with a twinkle in his eye.

Alys's chin tilted upward and she began to choose the words with which to dispute his assumption.

Before she could speak he held up his hand, as if to halt her harangue ere it began. "Children take the oddest notions, do they not? For example, their loathing of Mr. Pomeroy."

"Surely loathing is too strong a word. I realize they have not yet taken a liking to him, but they haven't truly been given the opportunity to know him. Besides, what reason could they have for not liking him?"

He looked at her queerly, as if she had asked the most nonsensical question. "Mr. Pomeroy and the girls have quietly declared war upon each other. Our esteemed scholar feels his dignity has been demeaned. He wants Sommerville to see that the little lasses are birched," he murmured, keeping an eye on Nelly as she wended her way about the room. "However, his lordship asserts that he is a gentleman and would never raise his hand to strike a lady, whether she be young or old."

"I commend him for his restraint," she murmured.

"Nevertheless, Pomeroy seems to be biding his time until the nanny is fit to do the birching herself."

Alys couldn't hide her expression of distress. "You must be mistaken! Mr. Pomeroy would not dare to instigate such cruelty... not to his own young cousins. He mustn't be allowed..." Her back stiffened with resolution. "I shall speak to him."

"You needn't put yourself in the way of his ire. It would be most unwise to do so at this time. For you see, the rubbings of the Stone are missing. He is thoroughly convinced that I am the villain responsible for *all* his misfortunes."

Was he jesting? Alys wondered. "Please, do not tease me with your jokes. What reason would Mr. Pomeroy have for accusing you so unjustly?"

"I laughed at him last night when he was short-sheeted."

"Short-sheeted? Oh dear, how dreadful," Alys murmured, then pressed her lips together, afraid she might snicker aloud. She reminded herself how shameful and disrespectful it was of her to be amused at the expense of poor Giles. She struggled briefly to discipline her expression before asking in a very polite tone, "And are you innocent of any involvement in these April Noddy high jinks?"

He looked only a little conscience-stricken. "I might have tipped one of the servants a crown and suggested that Mr. Pomeroy likes to sleep snug in his bed." His eyes twinkled, inviting her to share in his mirth. But she remained impervious to his cajolery. "The rubbings," he said, his brows drawing together in a frown, "are another matter altogether. Do you believe in following your instincts? I have learned never to doubt mine. Whenever I do, I always regret it." He thoughtfully stroked his chin. "I dare not dismiss my doubts concerning Signore Senusi and his henchman. Our two travellers from the Mediterranean are behaving in a curious fashion. They try to appear too innocent."

"But they are innocent. Mr. Pomeroy trusts them implicitly. Signore Senusi is renowned for his great knowledge of all things Egyptian."

His doubting expression seemed to scoff at her words, which were those so often heard from Mr. Pomeroy himself. "If you are determined to share all of the scholar's opinions...why even trouble to think for yourself?"

"Are you trying to provoke me, sir?"

"No, I am trying to help you see things as they are, not as you wish them to be. A wise hunter never follows the golden hind."

"Surely as a sportsman you know that the more difficult the struggle, the more highly prized the catch." She would not be turned from her course by a man who probably lived only for the exquisite moment of capture. "And I assure you that Mr. Pomeroy has everything that I require in a husband."

"Everything?" he snapped, a sceptical look shadowing his blue eyes.

For a moment her resolve weakened. Perhaps, just perhaps, Giles might lack a few qualities that would make their union perfect. He possessed definite ideas; did he believe that love had a place in matrimony? She realized there was much that she still had to discover about Giles.

"Aunt Alys, I found them!" Nelly, who'd quietly followed the trail of papers, called them from their conversation. "Look!" She pointed to her sisters standing in the doorway. Laughing, they tripped out and began to collect the bits of paper.

"Well done," Duncan said. "You've run the fox to earth." He glanced at Alys. "Patience and tenacity have won for her the prize. Nelly was not deceived by a false trail."

Alys cast him a challenging look. "And neither am I to be deceived."

"You shall be if you stubbornly pursue those notions that were ill-conceived from the beginning. Follow the honest inclinations of your heart."

"I daresay gentlemen hope that ladies will always give in to the promptings of emotion. Yet I've learned that to retain command of one's life one must rely upon the powers of good reasoning and thoughtful action."

He shook his head, as if pitying her. "Anyone who shuns emotion will never know what makes life worth living."

He appeared ready to elaborate further, but the entrance of Emma and a young maid, carrying a large tray, rendered him mute. What he did not convey in words, though, he intimated with his eyes. Alys had the distinct impression that sooner or later he would have much to say to her.

"I've brought the young ladies their dinner," Emma announced. She and the maid set out the girls' meal. "His lordship," Emma said, addressing herself to Duncan, "him knowing that you would understand the delicate situation in the library, wonders if you would mind very much taking a tray in your room. It would appear, sir, that the scholar is still up in the boughs about his bed and the missing papers." She winked at him. "You could take your repast with my lady. I'll just have another tray brought up at the time the young ladies are to retire."

Duncan glanced at Alys. "You needn't look so apprehensive. Perhaps you would feel more at ease in my company if you thought of me as the lasses do—as a member of the family. Or would you like your great-aunt Henrietta to serve as a chaperon?"

"Certainly not," Alys retorted. "Aunt Etta is sitting with Thea, who needs her more than I at the moment. Besides, McVicar makes for a very unpleasant dinner companion."

"He *does* lack that flare for conversation. He expresses himself poorly."

Alys held in her laughter with great difficulty. Yet the amusement in his eyes drew from her a smile.

He returned her smile, then offered his arm. "Shall we sit by the fire while we wait for the girls to finish their dinner?" He led her to the settle that sat at an angle before the schoolroom's small fireplace. She seated herself at one end and indicated that he should take his place at the other end. He did so, but slid over to the middle and stretched forth his hand towards the warmth of the fire.

She looked at him suspiciously.

"You needn't be worried, Miss Champion. Even a countrified fellow such as myself knows better than to make awkward advances upon a lady in the presence of five other females."

Her eyes widened.

"I was speaking of conversational advances." His blue eyes seemed to twinkle. "When next I choose to speak to you about a weighty matter I shall choose my moment more carefully. You will not be saved again by providential interruptions, for I shall know the right moment."

His words left her with little to say, but her thoughts churned as she tried to divine the import of his words. Instinctively she felt that there would be a significance to their next conversation that had heretofore been absent. This notion made her wary. She watched him as he silently stared at the flames dancing in the grate.

In no time their quiet corner of the schoolroom was overrun by the three Misses Pomeroy, nourished and eager to continue their games with *Uncle* Duncan before they had to retire.

Duncan obliged them by producing from the depths of his coat a top and a bit of string.

"Where did you get such a fine top?" Betsy asked.

He smiled and motioned for them to draw nearer. "It's a secret, but I daresay I can trust you. Did you know that your papa keeps it in a special drawer of his writing table? He let me borrow it. But we must take great care with it, for your papa has had it since he was a boy."

"Was Papa a little boy?" Nelly asked, her eyes brimming with astonishment.

The middle sister, whom they called Gaby, silently nudged her and frowned.

"Maybe Papa can come and play with us sometimes," Nelly said, with a grin of anticipation.

"Maybe," Duncan replied. "Your aunt Alys, a prime machinator of others' lives, would have the deed done without a by-your-leave." He looked at Alys. "Could you manage the feat?"

Alys took up the challenge. "If it can be done, I can do it. Can you say the same about that top?"

Chuckling, he wound the string round the toy and crouched down on the floor. With a jerk of the string, he set the top spinning across the room. The girls ran after it, clapping their hands excitedly.

Duncan moved behind Alys and leaned on the back of the settle. "Have you noticed that we both have an interest in helping others? Only our methods are at odds. If you saw a slow-moving river, you would want to change its course to hasten it on its way."

"And how would you get the river to flow properly?" she asked.

He was thoughtfully quiet for a moment. "I would study it, watching to see how it ebbed and flowed. Then, having discovered where the obstacle lay, I would *help* remove it. But I would not do all the work myself, for nothing becomes strong if it is never allowed to struggle on its own."

"But how does one stand by and watch even the weak grapple with the weighty matters of life?"

The girls returned with the top, and Duncan showed them how to wind the string and instructed them in how to set the top in motion. They happily went away to try for themselves. "Perhaps," he said, watching the girls, "the greatest service we can do for those we love is allow them to succeed or fail for themselves. Achievement has its own exquisite joy, which cannot be experienced if one never works for it. Would we know of Saint George if someone had slain the dragon for him?"

She looked at him in wonderment. How could a sportsman make that sort of thoughtful observation?

He flushed and laughed at himself. "I'm not a man of my word. I told you I would choose my moment with more care. I believe it must be the firelight that loosens my tongue. In my youth, we always had our best conversations before a fire. We would talk until the candles guttered out."

"You must have been a happy child." Alys felt a twinge of envy.

A smile that spoke of remembered times tugged at the corners of his mouth. "I once thought the good kinship in my family was the result of having an isolated estate, far removed from our neighbours. But as I advanced into manhood I noticed that our family was a wee bit unusual. The efforts wrought by my father and mother had forged bonds which, to this day, cannot be broken."

"You sound as if you long for your home in Northumberland."

"No, I long for a home of my own. I want to perpetuate those things that I enjoyed as a lad."

Alys fought the tug at her heart-strings. She stubbornly reminded herself that her choice had been made.

"I have stories within me just waiting to be told. Unfortunately, I have no little ones to tell them to." His blue eyes softened as he looked at her.

Betsy sidled up next to him. "Couldn't you make believe that we are your little girls . . . just for tonight? You could tell us a story. We like them! But Nanny

Jinks likes sermons. Couldn't you *please* make believe?''

Gaby and Nelly added their entreaties.

''Aunt Alys, you can make Uncle Duncan tell us a story,'' Nelly said, wheedling her way up onto Alys's lap and winding an arm about her neck.

Alys and Duncan looked at each other. She felt a softening begin to occur within her. She tried to halt it, but it was irrevocable. She hoped her resolve was not weakening.

The tender sparkle in his eyes could not be ignored. A cowardice she'd not suspected she possessed sent a shiver up her spine. What was happening to her?

''Please, Aunt Alys,'' Gaby said in her soft, shy voice.

''You are all a pack of wolves in sheep's clothing,'' Alys declared with a grudging smile. She decided to employ his method of removing obstacles, without trying to change the course of the flow. ''Mr. Todd, we entreat you, if you would be so kind, to favour us with a tale of daring deeds. As you are known in your family as a knight errant, this feat should not be above you.''

Duncan pushed away from the back of the settle and placed a chair next to the fire. ''Tis an observance of tradition for the story-teller to take the place of honour by the warm glow of the fire.'' He sat down, crossing one booted foot over the other. His gaze travelled from Alys to the flames.

Nelly chose to sit at his feet, with her elbows resting on the knees of her folded legs and her chin propped on her fists. Betsy and Gaby took their places next to their aunt.

The room grew expectantly quiet.

"Far away and long ago, in the resplendent Kingdom of Sterlington, the people were happy and prosperous. Whenever it rained there it was a merry shower which always ended with a bright, colourful rainbow. The children of the kingdom were especially cheerful and kind hearted." He smiled down at Nelly. "There were three young ladies who waited upon the royal princess. Their names were Lady Elizabeth, Lady Gabriella, and Lady Eleanor. Lady Elizabeth saw to the princess's safety by performing many brave deeds. Lady Gabriella made sure that the princess was never bored or out of sorts by reading or singing to her."

"What did Lady Eleanor do?" asked Nelly, with wide, eager eyes.

"She played games with the princess," Duncan replied.

"What was the princess's name?" Gaby asked in her quiet way.

Before he could answer Alys cautioned the girls not to interrupt further.

Duncan looked at her with an amused twinkle. "The princess was known as Her Royal Highness Princess Alice. She was the beauty of the kingdom, for her fair tresses were as soft as a whisper and her blue eyes as clear as the sky on a spring day. But, for a reason that none could understand, she had not married. She was waiting for her prince to find her.''

"Did she wait as long as Aunt Alys?" Nelly asked innocently.

"Almost as long," he replied. "But while she waited, she and the three young ladies had many adventures.'' He went on to weave a tale about an evil elf and the daring deeds of the three brave lasses, holding the girls spellbound with each word. "But their adventure with the evil elf could not compare to that of the Black Witch. The Black Witch had a wicked heart and she hated happiness. When the witch heard of the Kingdom of Sterlington she sent her imps, the blue devils, to make trouble. They painted everything in the kingdom blue, even the princess's hair. The happy people became sad. The blue devils stayed with them, and even the princess cried to be rescued.''

Alys cast him a doubtful look.

"All the neighbouring kingdoms heard about the land of blue," he said, continuing with the tale, "and they feared that their land, too, would become blue. The kings all decided to send their best knights to vanquish the blue devils. One by one, the knights were defeated by the witch's imps. Then, from a land far away to the north, came a knight errant. He rode a white charger and his armour was as gleaming bright as the noonday sun. His helmet was as shiny as a mirror.''

"He sounds blindingly bright," Alys remarked.

"Just so," Duncan murmured.

"*Shh,*" the girls hissed in unison.

"What happened next?" Betsy asked. "Was the knight errant able to defeat the blue devils?"

Duncan paused, then looked up as Emma emerged from the connecting bedchamber. With a nightgown draped over her arm, she waited expectantly by the door. "I suspect," he said, "that we shall have to wait until tomorrow to find out if the knight was successful."

After a few strong protests and repining sighs, the girls trailed into the bedchamber and dolefully closed the door behind them.

Left alone, Duncan and Alys fell quiet for moment. She wondered about this man who possessed such a curious mix of talents and interests.

"You have quite a remarkable way with children, sir. How do you come by your charm?"

He chuckled to himself. "When a man has a horde of nieces and nephews of his own he must either recall the fancies of his youth or learn to ignore the rapscallions."

The young nursery maid entered with their dinner tray and quietly went about setting out their meal.

"Perhaps you could regale me with those fancies of your youth while we dine," Alys said, rising from the settle. "But first let me bid the girls a good-night."

After she rejoined him the time seemed to have wings as they conversed and gradually exchanged memories of their youth. They discovered a common fondness for fairy tales. When the covers were removed they lingered at the small nursery table, telling each other the tales they loved the most.

Enjoying his deep-timbred voice and his north-country dialect, Alys could have cheerfully listened to him all night long. But as the night deepened, she became very much aware of the impropriety of their situation. She eased her conscience by assuring herself that the presence of Emma in the next room lent a small portion of respectability to their continued companionship.

Finally, as the fire burned low and the candles began to flicker, Alys rose and excused herself. She called for Emma. When her maid did not respond, she wondered aloud, "Has she drifted off to sleep?"

"I suspect that she has slipped off to walk out with my man Charles. The young nursery maid is the one you'd likely find asleep in the trundle bed."

"Emma and your man are—" She gulped on the words that would not come.

He smiled at her discomfort. "You needn't look so distressed. Charles is an upright man. He'll be quite a challenge for your Emma. Ah, but I was forgetting how mistress and maid both relish defying all opposition."

With a defiant tilt of her chin, she began to bid him good-night.

"Don't let the blue devils get you," he said with a curious gleam in his eyes.

Though she was halfway to the door, she stopped and came back to him. "How ever will you bring about a satisfactory ending to your tale?"

"Would you like to know?" Duncan looked at her for what seemed a very long time, then he took her by the hand. She came close to him as if mesmerized. They stood facing each other.

"After vanquishing all his foes—those impish blue devils—" he said softly, "the knight errant came to the royal princess for his reward."

He looked deep into her eyes, as if to the depths of her soul, and found there the response he desired. He raised her hand and placed it on his chest. "The princess felt the knight's heart beat for her. She knew what she must give him. But our princess had placed a guard about her heart. Only she could give the command that would unbar the way. With great courage, she came to him." He put one hand at the small of Alys's back and drew her near. "The knight took her in his arms."

Her eyes closed.

"There are many sweet kisses, but none so sweet as the first." His lips brushed over her ear and he murmured her name. "He gave to her his first kiss of true love."

Duncan kissed her deeply, as if he would draw the very life from her body.

CHAPTER SEVEN

ALYS CLUTCHED one of the lapels of Duncan's coat, feeling quite weak in the knees. She marvelled that one's heart could beat so fast without one having run a great distance. She felt frightened by the surge of sensations coursing through her. Never had she felt so alive. How could a man's lips be so inviting...so stimulating? As he deepened the kiss, any inclination for rational thought gave way to the onslaught of a hitherto unknown passion.

At last they broke from each other. He looked ready to take her lips once again. She gazed at him with uncertain eyes. The hand that had before clutched his coat now abruptly stiffened and pushed him back, holding him at a distance.

Unanswerable questions flashed through her mind. Should she strike him? Why had he kissed her with such intensity? Where had the furious passion within her come from? Was she a wanton? How could she have a tendre for one man and then be stirred to a remarkable degree by another? Was it merely the excitement of her first kiss?

Finally, after seven-and-twenty years, she'd been kissed. No one had ever before dared take the liberty. She wondered if the second kiss would have the same effect.

The hand that held him off suddenly drew him to her. With a questioning gaze she looked into his eyes—such deep blue eyes. Her lashes lowered as his lips closed over hers.

She felt the flame within her leap higher, and at the same time burn deeper. She was lost, yet she felt safe. She moved closer to the keeper of the flame.

A small moan escaped her as his lips moved from her mouth to her ear. "Alys, my dearest girl," he whispered, between kisses on her temple, "should this continue... one of us will be... thoroughly compromised."

She jerked away from him. A feeling of great disquiet overcame her. She was supposed to be in love with Giles. He'd been her heart's desire for eight years. Why had she behaved with such a want of decorum with Duncan? "What have I done?" she cried, her eyes wide with shock.

Duncan grinned in a slow, soft manner. "You kissed me."

"Oh, this is dreadful! Whatever came over me?"

He looked at her with a warm glow in his eyes. "Perhaps you were held spellbound. I'm said to be a dream weaver."

She clutched her hands protectively over her heart. "You are a sly-boots. You...you were to teach me the art of the hunt, not practise the art upon me."

"Often to learn one must do." His voice had a strange, tight quality, one she'd never heard before. "You are a most able student, Miss Champion. Now that you've been taught, you can dashed well kiss your stoic scholar."

"What will Giles think should he discover—" Why was Duncan glowering at her so fiercely?

"Do you think you have been sullied to the point of ruination? Let me assure you that your virtue has not been compromised. None the less, should Mr. Pomeroy desire satisfaction, I shall be happy to meet him whenever it pleases him."

He looked as if it would please him greatly to put a period to Giles's existence. "No, no, that won't be necessary. It was merely a kiss." She needed to see Giles. Surely a kiss from *him* would drive away the treacherous emotions within her.

Duncan turned from her and stared into the dying embers of the fire, clutching the mantel as if for support.

Alys gazed at him, wanting to give him comfort. How had she hurt him? He knew that she loved Giles. He knew that she was intent upon marrying the man for whom she'd waited so long. Surely Duncan had no real liking for her—he teased her, they had nothing in common and he often said the most outrageous things to her. A tender smile came to her lips and with it a burning glow of tears to her eyes. No one had ever suspected she possessed hidden fires, not until Duncan had made the discovery. In a very short time he'd found the most glorious things within her.

But it was all a game to him, wasn't it?

She began to repeat to herself that she loved Giles, and for a few moments she again felt in command of her world. Then her mind seemed to spin with the words *I love Giles*.

In a state of confusion, she hurried to the door and fled for her safe harbour—the library—and the reassuring presence of her beloved.

AS THE LIBRARY CLOCK chimed the hour of midnight, Giles Pomeroy finished his bitter-tasting tea and leant back in his chair. "How very odd. I feel decidedly more drowsy."

"You have laboured many long hours," a muted voice said from the shadows beyond the candlelight. "Sleep is needed. A soft bed, feather-filled pillows and warm blankets, await you. The peace of a night's slumber will refresh you. Sleep. Sleep. Sleep is what you want." The hypnotic voice coaxed Giles's eyes to close.

For several minutes uninterrupted silence reigned in the library, until the sounds of deepening sleep began to build. Giles awakened himself when he gasped for breath during a particularly loud snore. He yawned and wiped the slobber from his chin.

"Must have dozed off," Giles mumbled sleepily. "Must beg your pardon for being—" he yawned and stretched "—for being so rude. I should retire." He dragged himself to his feet and tottered.

"Allow me to see you to your chamber." Senusi came forward out of the shadows. "I, too, wish to seek my bed." He nodded to Baka and murmured, "Get the ox-cart." In no time he had Giles safely tucked in bed, and then he stealthily returned to the darkened library, making sure that the rest of the house had settled for the night.

Senusi found Baka trying to push the stone-laden manger across the floor. "I watched the footmen and the carriers bring the Stone into the house," Senusi whispered as he drew nearer to his commander. "Four exceedingly large men were needed to move and lift it. Your strength, though mighty, will not be enough. But be not cast down, for the Roll of Fate has said, 'Be not discouraged by adverse circumstances.'"

Baka rose from his crouched position and wiped the moisture from his brow. "If I were not bound and chafed by these vile trappings, I could move more freely." He tried unsuccessfully to flex the muscles of his back. "The English have fashioned the coats of their servants for bowing and scraping." With one great movement, he rent the back seam of his jacket. "*Now* let us take the Stone home."

"Noble Baka, I believe you capable of any task," Senusi said, shrugging out of his coat and divesting himself of his waistcoat, "but we must use our heads as well as our hands. Where are the ropes and the smooth poles that I asked you to prepare?"

Going to a large, open window at one end of the library, Baka leaned out and, from the ox-cart which stood waiting just outside, produced the needed items. Using a method practised by the ancients, they eased the Stone onto the poles, which lay close to each other. As they slowly pushed the Stone across the floor the poles rolled beneath it, causing a great rumbling sound like distant thunder. Often they stopped for Senusi to move one pole from the rear and place it in front of the others.

As ALYS DESCENDED the stairs, she noticed how still and dark it was. Not a servant lingered anywhere in sight, not a taper burned to give light. She had not realized how advanced the hour had become. The entire household seemed to have retired for the night. But she recalled Giles's habit of studying into the wee hours of the morning and took heart that a rendezvous with him was just what she desired. He would never take her in his arms if the other gentlemen were present.

Slowly moving through the darkness, she wondered what pretext she could give for coming down so late. And she must have some excuse, else he might think she was throwing herself at his head. A book seemed plausible. She would tell him she could not sleep and ask if he would recommend a book for her.

BAKA AND SENUSI stopped before the low edge of the large windowsill. Here the ropes were employed, but even the combined efforts of the two men were insufficient to lift the Stone over the sill. The Noble Baka was about to recruit the mighty strength of the ox when Senusi pushed him down behind a low-backed sofa.

"Listen," whispered the younger man.

A gentle knock repeated, then the door eased open. The shadowy form of a woman precipitously entered, as if assured of her welcome. Then she came to an abrupt halt and her shoulders drooped.

For a moment Senusi thought she would go away, but she turned and began to look about. The instinct of a born womanizer alerted him that his goal was within his reach. A recent reading of the Roll of Fate flashed through his mind: "Contentment is a richer treasure than any other to be found." He knew that in Miss Champion's arms he would find a man's greatest contentment. Possessing her had become more important to him than taking possession of the Stone.

For the moment the Stone would have to wait. Their presence in the library would soon be discovered. He watched her move slowly to the open window and he knew that he must take action soon or lose his opportunity.

THE DARKNESS OF THE ROOM overwhelmed Alys and her tentative smile fell away. No sight of Giles greeted her. Why had she thought Fate would favour her? Her shoulders drooped. Giles must be soundly sleeping in his bed, dreaming, no doubt, about his blasted stone.

She sent a scathing glance to the place of honour in which the rock had reposed since its arrival. How strange... She peered through the gloom. Where was it? *The Stone was gone.*

For days she'd nearly tripped over the Stone every time she'd entered the library. In the dark its placement seemed different from what she'd remembered.

There it sat before the long window, as if out of sorts for being dislodged from its position. At the sight of the ropes fastened to the Stone, a sensation of alarm crept up Alys's spine. She took a step back, intent upon alerting someone about the unusual occurrence. It was then that she sensed she was not alone in the room. She heard movement, but before she could react, something was thrown over her head, making the darkness complete. A pair of arms fastened about her, a hand going over her mouth.

SENUSI WISHED IT WERE his lips instead of his hand that was pressed over her mouth. She squirmed against him, and he thought he would perish from the pleasure this movement evoked.

In his native tongue, he murmured words of passion into her ear. He pressed against her, feeling quite sure that his ardour would be welcomed.

She stilled abruptly. He felt encouraged and eased his hold upon her, intent upon turning her about and feasting upon her ripe lips.

With his eyes half closed, his body yearning to release the pent-up ache of wanting her, his senses failed to perceive the threat which rose before him. Lashing out blindly, she struck him with such force that he reeled back, his cheek burning as if scorched.

Baka shoved past him and pushed the screaming hell-cat into the draperies, wrapping them about her in cocoonlike fashion. He used some lengths of rope to secure her in her damask prison. Her cries were muffled by the thick cloth.

Cursing Senusi and calling him seven kinds of a fool, the Noble Baka stalked about in a towering rage.

Senusi tried to explain that he had only been attempting to subdue the woman.

"Be still!" the Noble Baka bellowed. "If you must speak, do so in our tongue, lest this woman discover who we are." He looked at the Stone and ground his teeth. "So near to success, yet because of the fire in your loins we must withdraw."

"I shall read the Roll of Fate once again. Perhaps this is not our time. Perhaps Ra wishes to test our devotion and patience."

"Perhaps Ra will rob you of your manhood and make of you a woman. Then, by the gods, as a woman you will know the curse of men like yourself." Baka grabbed Senusi's waistcoat and coat and flung them at him. "Come, her screams may have awakened the house. I must hide the ox-cart before it is discovered."

They left the library like shadows of the night.

DUNCAN PAUSED before the door of his bedchamber. He was tempted to turn round and go below to the library to see for himself if Giles had kissed Alys to her satisfaction. It was a slight comfort to be unable to conjure up the image of the scholar as a flourishing swain.

Yet no amount of solace could eradicate the memory of Alys's rejection. She'd fled from him as a vixen before the hounds of hell.

He chided himself for having driven her too quickly. None the less the second kiss had been given, not taken. She might have come to him desiring an answer to a question that only she knew, but she had come, freely and of her own volition.

Alys had given him much more than a kiss. She'd given him an unspoken promise: she would come to him again.

He smiled to himself. His mother's words of wisdom seemed to come to his memory at the most unexpected times. He could almost hear her saying, just as she had done long ago when he was learning to ride, "Patience is the best remedy for every trouble. You must fail before you can succeed. Try again, my son."

Alys Champion would be his, regardless of a silly scholar or any other piddling obstacle.

Humming an old hunting air, he began to make ready for bed. It was his custom to sleep in the state of Adam's innocence. Duncan was about to remove his breeches when a noise carried to his ears. It sounded like furniture turning over. He slipped his shirt back on and made for the door, grabbing his boots as he went.

From the library came faint, muffled calls for help. Duncan burst into the room. Soft moonlight streamed through a window, now bare of its draperies. Something moved in the heap of damask at the foot of the sill.

Sensing that any threat of danger had passed, Duncan advanced quickly upon the fallen draperies. "Mr. Pomeroy? Don't move, sir. How the deuce did these ropes come to be wrapped about you?" He felt a knot and sat back on his heels. "Who—? What strange goings-on have occurred here?" The blond head that popped up from the parted draperies took Duncan back. "Alys! My girl, have you been harmed?"

"He—he—he grabbed me and—he touched me!" She leaned against him and buried her head in his shoulder, as if needing his strength and comfort.

The bestial behaviour she described didn't sound at all like Pomeroy, but none the less Duncan wanted to plant him a facer. The fribble should have protected her with his life. Duncan's jaw tightened. Whoever had molested her would pay for his infamy.

"Did you see who—" He had to master his mounting rage. He wanted to break someone in half, but he didn't want to upset her further. "—who seized you?"

Without lifting her head, she shook it and sniffed dolefully.

He held her close to him and stroked her hair. Her fair curls gleamed in the moonlight. He felt deeply sad that the circumstances were such that to offer her a compliment would be a grave offence. She'd endured an unthinkable ordeal at the hands of one man and what she needed now was consolation.

He pressed his cheek against the crown of her head and rubbed her back with soothing caresses.

"Why is your touch so different from other men's?" she murmured against his chest.

He stroked her jaw. "Someday you shall find the answer." *And then your hunt will be at an end*, he added to himself. He eased her back from him. "If you are sufficiently recovered, I think I ought to ring for the servants and have Lord Sommerville awakened. He would want to be informed of any incident that resulted in harm to his kith or kin."

In that silent way that servants have of conveying news to an entire household, every adult residing in Green Hill House was soon roused from their sleep and informed that Miss Champion had been waylaid in the library. Sommerville and his lady, who would not stay abed, came down, and all their guests emerged from their rooms and followed after them, Giles staggering along at the rear. They gathered round Alys with a torrent of questions and outraged comments.

Giles gingerly made his way to a chair and sat down, holding his head. He seemed to have difficulty keeping his eyes open.

"Please, everyone," Sommerville said with an air of authority, "allow me to question my sister-in-law. She has already suffered enough. She needn't suffer more at our hands. Now, Alys, tell us what you can."

She bit her lip and glanced from Giles to Duncan, who stood beside her with his hand resting upon the chair-back close to her shoulder. Duncan gave her a reassuring smile. Giles did not appear to be attending closely to what was transpiring.

Slowly she recounted her tale. "I came down for a—a book. The hour was quite advanced. I noticed after entering the library that—that things were not as they should be. I was about to leave—I think I intended to alert someone. . . ." She looked up at Duncan for a moment, then closed her eyes. "As I turned to go...*he* grabbed me."

"Who?" Sommerville asked in a soft, compassionate voice.

Alys shook her head. "I could not see him. He caught me from behind. He—he held me to him. His breath was hot and foul-smelling."

Senusi cupped his hand and puffed into it, then stepped back from the tight circle of listeners.

"He said things to me," Alys continued. "But I could not understand him. He spoke strangely."

"Aha! A Gypsy," exclaimed Great-Aunt Etta.

Thea cried out and clutched Sommerville's hand. "My dearest Alys, how dreadful! Did he—did he try to force his attentions upon you?"

"Yes." It was spoken in a whisper. Then Alys's head came up proudly. "But he failed and, for his impudence, he received a good boxing of the ears. My hand still hurts from it."

Senusi turned away from the light of the candelabra.

"The fellow was no better than an animal," Sommerville declared. "The constable must be sent for."

"Damnation!" Giles gasped in a strangled voice. He abruptly sat up, as if awaking from a nightmare, and pointed to the vacant space where the Stone had sat. "Mr. Todd, what have you done with it? Where is it? What has happened here?"

"Daft," Great-Aunt Etta muttered, shaking her head and giving Giles a pitying look. "Young man, have you not been attending? My niece has suffered at the hands of a thorough scoundrel—a Gypsy. We do not know *where* he is hiding, but no stone shall remain unturned in our search for him."

Giles ran his hand through his hair and held his head at the temples.

"Demented," reasserted Etta. "Sommerville, he's not fit company for Thea in her delicate condition. The babe is likely to be as brainsick as this young man. It will be said that bad blood runs in your family."

"Look!" Giles cried. "The Stone—"

The old woman put a quizzing glass to her eye and stared in the direction that Giles pointed. "He even sees things that are not there."

"It is gone!" Giles sank to the floor.

"Pomeroy, don't you dare faint!" Sommerville stepped forward and grabbed his cousin by the scruff of the neck.

Duncan laid his hand on Alys's shoulder. "My dear, do you know what has happened to the relic?"

She pointed to the heap of damask. "It's there in the draperies. I noticed that the Stone was missing. It was then that I was attacked. I must have interrupted their work. There were two or three very strong men. They may have been Gypsies, but, as I said, I could not see their faces. I only heard them speak."

"You," Giles cried, looking at her with wondering eyes, "you foiled their evil designs. You saved the Stone! How splendid! How brave!"

"How foolish," inserted Duncan, frowning at Alys.

Giles rushed to the Stone with a spring in his step. He swept the draperies aside and embraced the antiquity. "Miss Champion, you are a true heroine. To risk your life for something of greater value..." He swallowed, appearing to be overcome by some manly emotion that could not be expressed. "The Stone is safe. You have earned my unceasing gratitude. Of course, it is quite distressing that an Englishwoman should be waylaid in the home of her nearest and dearest. Indeed, anyone with an ounce of proper feelings would be moved by your plight. The villain must have been all about in his head to think he could get away with such a prize." He smiled at Alys, then tenderly stroked the smooth black face of the Stone. "But she's safe now."

"No slab of stone is worth a *lady's* safety, Pomeroy," Duncan said quietly. With narrowed eyes, his gaze fell upon Senusi. The foreigner had squirmed during Alys's recounting. He kept his face out of the light. What was he attempting to hide? A large, red welt on his cheek? "Signore Senusi, you have said little. What is your opinion of this dastard who attacked a defenceless lady?"

Senusi stepped farther into the shadows. "He must have been tempted by Miss Champion's beauty. Who can blame a man for desiring to touch a white rose?"

A snort came from the side of the room. Duncan looked over and saw Baka standing by the wall next to the door. The manservant folded his arms over his chest and disdainfully ignored everyone.

Duncan glanced from the manservant to the master. He watched Senusi hang his head. Here was a man who felt shame. Here was a man who was fully dressed in the middle of the night, while nearly everyone else was in some state of *déshabillé*. Surely Senusi was a man with a guilty secret. He needed to be asked a few particular questions.

"*Signore,* I must assume that you have not yet retired for the night," Duncan said. "What has kept you from seeking your bed?"

"He went up when I did," Giles interposed. "I daresay he must have fallen asleep in his clothes."

"Did you see any Gypsies roaming about, *signore?*" Duncan would not be turned from his course. "Where were you when Miss Champion was attacked in the dark?"

Giles raked a hand through his long locks. "Blister it, sir, your impudence is not to be tolerated. Instead of cross-questioning an innocent man, why not seek out the real culprits? Sommerville, we must have a pair of stout footmen stand guard. This band of Gypsy thieves will no doubt return for the Stone."

"Signore," Duncan said, his gaze never once having deviated from the face of Senusi, "is that a welt on your cheek?"

Senusi's hand crept to cover his cheek. "Ah—an unwilling housemaid—"

"Oh!" cried Thea. Her exclamation became a groan. "Edmund!" She reached for her husband, then bent over in evident pain. "Alys," she called as she tried to catch her breath. "Alys... help me."

CHAPTER EIGHT

ALYS CHAMPION RAISED the hem of her morning gown as she hurried down the candle-lit marble staircase. She quickly crossed the entrance hall; then, listening intently, she hastened towards the sound of masculine voices carrying from the rear rooms of the villa.

She hesitated just outside the library. Though still recent, the memories of being accosted were fast receding. She squared her shoulders, pushed back a wisp of fine blond hair and pinched her wan cheeks a few times to bring colour to them. Regardless of the urgency of her errand, she was determined to present a pleasing appearance. She tapped on the door before quietly entering.

Sommerville stood with his back to her, apparently unaware that she had entered. He appeared absorbed in his contemplation of the large black stone which had been moved again to its place of importance.

Giles stood next to him and was even more caught up in his study of the Stone. "A fortnight is hardly long enough for a proper examination," he said, frowning. "Sommerville, could you request that we keep it just a while longer? Sommerville?"

His lordship started when his cousin's voice rose in volume. "Were you speaking to me, Giles? I must apologize. I was deep in my own thoughts."

"I understand completely. It is a captivating piece of antiquity. Which is why you must insist that we be allowed to extend the time for our studies of it."

"A fortnight is sufficient to make a plaster cast of the Stone," observed Sommerville, "and take a few more rubbings of it. Then you may study the copy at your leisure. As a scholar of some repute, you should have no trouble deciphering the texts. I expect great things of you, Giles. Pray do not disappoint me." His words seemed to recall a pressing matter to him. He pulled his timepiece from his waistcoat pocket. Tapping impatiently on the face of the watch, he murmured, "What can be taking her so long?"

Giles did not respond. His whole attention was again caught up in the Stone.

"Sommerville," Alys called softly, coming up behind him. When he turned, she could see that he was in a sad state. "It won't be long now."

"It has been all of five hours." Sommerville gazed at her, his eyes shadowed with worry. His usual neat appearance had deteriorated with the passing of each hour. The points of his collar drooped and his neck-cloth looked mangled. "If it is much longer I shall go mad." He began to pace, and his quick stride brought him back to her in a very few moments.

"According to *Dr. Wingate*," she said, purposefully adding emphasis to the physician's name to catch Sommerville's attention, "you may rest easy within the hour." She smiled at his relieved expression. He was like most men, who paid more heed to a man's opinion than a woman's. "And," she added with a twinkle, "Aunt Etta and the midwife, who are also attending her, concur with him."

"Is Thea in much pain?" he asked before he stepped away from her once more and continued with his route across the room.

Alys found his question a rather awkward one to answer. Distress seemed to be an unavoidable part of a woman's lying-in. "Thea is in fine spirits, considering her delicate situation, and seems to be..." She paused, groping for the proper refinement of words. "Er—she's managing her travail with great fortitude and surprising strength. You mustn't worry so about her. Truly, she's faring quite well." In an attempt to give him some consolation, she joined him in his pacing. With just a touch she managed to slow his progress and bring him in step with her, though her long legs could have matched his stride.

Sommerville stopped abruptly and clasped her hand, then whispered, "You cannot know how this waiting is for me. No one does. Every time she's been confined I fear—I *greatly* fear that death may claim her.''

"You mustn't think such thoughts," she said.

"There's no help for it. One would suppose that after the birth of three fine daughters I'd learn to be more composed. But each time the waiting is worse than before."

Alys suppressed her own fears. Her brother-in-law clearly needed her, and she always felt a great contentment when she was needed. For the moment she would be his support. She took his arm and continued to walk by his side, listening to his worries.

"She doesn't know," he said, his voice low and raw, "how very fond of her I am. I never tell her in words. It seems rather improper to speak of such things to one's wife."

Alys glanced at Giles and wondered if he shared his cousin's sentiments on the proper comportment of married couples.

"Your father, God rest him," Sommerville continued in a rambling manner, "thought I had wed Thea as a matter of business or convenience." He grasped Alys's hand tightly. "It wasn't that way. I loved her to distraction. But I've never been able to tell her. If she should die . . ."

"She will not die, I promise you. Everyone in our family has amazingly good health. Great-Aunt Etta is in fine fettle and she's all of seventy." Alys thought it best to refrain from reminding him that her dear mama had died of grief, or so the doctors said. And three years before that unhappy day, her father had succumbed to a severe case of inflammation of the lungs. The recital of these past misfortunes would hardly cheer him or give him hope.

"I'll never love anyone as much as I love Thea," Sommerville whispered.

Alys let her gaze wander to Giles, whose long brown hair fell over his serious eyes as he continued to examine the Stone. Would he ever love her with such devotion? She sighed, and then rebuked herself for letting her thoughts stray from Sommerville's concerns. "But surely you hold a great affection for your little girls."

"The esteem for one's children is quite different than that for one's wife. Should you ever marry you'll know that exquisite difference." His lordship paused, then grimaced. "Er, pray forgive me. I daresay at seven-and-twenty there's a chance that you may still..."

She stiffened and flushed, hoping that Giles's attention remained with the antiquity.

Sommerville groaned. "I am making a muddle of this. It's the worry. My mind is so filled with it that I'm not fit company for a lady."

"You needn't concern yourself with me. I *am* known as a thick-skinned old maid. But I do...not repine," she said, her words tripping on the lie, "and neither should you about Thea. I must return now.

She may have need of me. Perhaps Mr. Pomeroy could interest you in a game of chess." She turned and called to the scholar, then, smiling at her brother-in-law, she called again. "Oh, Mr. Pomeroy!"

"I beg your pardon," Giles said in his distracted manner. His eyes lingered on the Stone for a few seconds longer, then, tossing his hair back from his brow, he turned his wandering attention on her. "Miss Champion, when did you come down?" Before she could reply he said, "It doesn't matter. Look! She is back where she belongs and, though she was handled roughly, she has not sustained a mark or injury. Our treasured Rosetta Stone shall remain under guard, though. If only she could linger with us for a while longer." He turned enthusiastically to Alys. "Surely if you asked his lordship to extend his influence—"

"Sommerville is greatly worried at the moment," she said.

"He need not worry about the Stone," Giles said, placing his arm protectively about it. "I am here to see that she comes to no harm"

"Mr. Pomeroy, you must attend more closely." Alys couldn't keep the exasperation from her voice.

"I assure you that I shall not fall asleep at my post." He took up his position with a great deal of ceremony.

Alys had to take herself in hand to keep from boxing the zealous antiquarian's ears. How could an intelligent man be so addle-pated?

"Might I be of assistance, Miss Champion?" Duncan said from the doorway. "A game of billiards is what's needed. Come along, Ned. We are keeping this lady from important matters." He smiled at Alys in a way that left her light-hearted.

"LADY SOMMERVILLE," said Dr. Wingate in his prosaic way, "you may now bear down." He looked pointedly at Alys. "Tell her ladyship to push with all her might and strength."

Alys gave Thea the command.

"I realize," Dr. Wingate continued in his slow, deliberate manner, "that ladies are not supposed to have any strength, but I have observed that they are divinely imbued with it at the time of birthing. I've seen a female splinter the post off a bed in the throes of her supreme exigency. The female of whom I speak is a very large woman, of course, built for giving birth. Has nine babes and is due to bring another into the world in the early summer." He paused and inspected the progress of his patient. "Miss Champion—really, an unmarried female shouldn't be present. Won't you reconsider? No? I thought not. Well, miss, would you tell her ladyship to push quite hard this time? I don't believe she's doing her duty."

Alys glared at the doctor, then turned her attention to her sister. Alys began to relay the doctor's command, but was forestalled.

"Tell Dr. Wingate that I *am* doing my duty," Thea said succinctly, between clenched teeth. "Tell him to do *his* duty and cease his prattling."

"Miss Champion," the doctor said, his tone condescending, "pray enquire of her ladyship whether she desires an opiate elixir. Many women need it to calm their hysterics."

Thea pulled Alys down to her and whispered, "Do not let him give me any laudanum. I cannot abide it. And ... and don't tell Edmund that I was so cross. He mustn't ever know that I was anything other than his perfect wife." She grimaced ferociously and pushed down for a long moment. Panting and glistening from her efforts, she tugged on Alys's hand.

Alys leaned down, and in doing so tried to loosen her sister's grip just a little. "Take some deep breaths, dearest. Try to be easy until it comes again. Any moment now and you'll have a new babe to coo over." She received a stern look from the doctor for her impudence in trespassing upon his field of expertise.

"If anything should ..." whispered Thea. "Please tell Edmund that I loved him. I do not believe he knows."

Alys struggled with her conscience. Surely she could tell Sommerville and Thea of their devotion for each other. She could set matters right for them. Yet if she did, they would never know the exquisite joy of discovering their love by themselves. No, *they* would have to declare themselves.

How odd that she should abandon her usual manner of management in favour of merely assisting. She wondered whether it had something to do with Duncan's influence upon her.

"Alys, promise to tell him," Thea rasped out. An awful groan tore from her and she bore down hard.

"Rest easy," Alys said. "I will do what I can."

Old Peony Dinwiddie, received by all as the village sage and midwife, nudged in next to the doctor. She clasped her hands over her midriff, where her sagging breasts and rounded stomach joined in one large curve. Then, glancing up, she gave Lady Sommerville a motherly smile. "You'll be feelin' better soon. Have you another push you can give us? That's the way!"

Great-Aunt Henrietta glanced over their shoulders. "How exciting. Doctor, I hope you'll have the goodness to deliver a boy."

Dr. Wingate glared at her. "There are far too many females in this room!" He edged the midwife out of the way.

"Who are you suggestin' to leave?" asked Old Peony. "Her ladyship, I suppose?" She peered over his shoulder. "The babe's acomin'!"

The good doctor looked down his nose at her, then announced, "The infant is about to enter the world. Miss Champion, be so good as to request that her ladyship refrain from bearing down for a moment." Methodically he went to work. "You—" he glanced at Old Peony "—come lend a hand—a clean hand. I cannot abide dirt.'' He glanced at her hands then grunted his approval. ''Miss Champion! Her ladyship's pushing.''

Thea looked helplessly at Alys in a manner that seemed to ask how she was to hold back a rushing tide. Without an answer to give her, Alys just shrugged and told her to catch her breath.

''That's just what she should do,'' commented Old Peony as she closely watched the progress of the birth. ''Say what you will, *phyzician,* I've got the touch. And a good ironing out can save a woman from death.''

Alys's arm, where Thea grasped it, felt as if it were maimed. The fabric on the sleeve had given way beneath the onslaught of Thea's fingernails.

''Let us be thankful,'' Great-Aunt Etta remarked cheerfully as she glanced at the clock, ''that the child had the good sense to hold off coming until the Sabbath dawned. 'Saturday's child has a journey to go, but the child that is born on the Sabbath Day is happy and loving, good and gay.' ''

''Hold your chatter,'' ordered Dr. Wingate. ''Miss Champion, tell her ladyship that she may now push once more.''

''Here comes the babe!''

Alys's attention shifted from her sister to the doctor and back again to Thea. Events were occurring so fast that she hardly knew what was happening, until the midwife bundled the squalling infant and sang praises to heaven. "A boy! How pleased his lordship will be."

The doctor handed Alys a cup. "Give this to her ladyship. It's a sleeping draught."

Setting it aside, Alys glanced at Thea, who looked exhausted and ready to sleep without the need of medication. Alys faced Dr. Wingate defiantly. "My sister, as well you know, cannot abide laudanum. She insisted I be here to see that you not dose her with any strong potions."

"It shall be as her ladyship wishes," he said stiffly. "But let the consequences be upon your head, not hers." He haughtily turned away and continued with his work. "If you wish to be useful, Miss Champion, you might go to his lordship and impart the news of the birth . . . and also inform him that her ladyship is doing as well as can be expected. She may receive him after a few hours' rest."

Alys kissed her sister's cheek and eased from her grasp. Then, heartened by the sounds of a lusty cry, she left the room and rushed down to the antechamber connected to the library.

Without preamble, she burst into the room and announced, "Edmund, you've an heir! A fine, healthy son."

Sommerville stood by the billiard table barely breathing. He dropped his cue stick and asked, "And Thea? Does she . . . live?"

"Yes," she answered gently. "Dr. Wingate has said you may see her after she's recovered sufficiently. She did very well. And she's given you a son." A tear came to her eye and she wiped it briskly away.

Duncan clapped Sommerville on the back and they laughed together. "Rouse the house, Ned. We must drink a toast to your new son."

Drawn into the room by the commotion, Giles looked about in a dumbfounded manner until he discovered the source of the celebration. "This *is* a happy day," he exclaimed. "First, the Stone is saved and now the arrival of a new heir. We must announce it to the world. I daresay a discreet disclosure to the *Times* and the *Gazette* would do nicely."

Sommerville said, "Giles, summon the servants. Have the church bells rung. Send messengers to all our relations and friends, telling them of the birth and inviting them to the christening."

"Surely there is no need for such haste?" Alys quizzed him with a gentle smile.

Flushing slightly, his lordship replied, "I dare not trifle with Fate. Though I'm not overly superstitious about evil spirits encroaching upon the child, I believe the customs must be observed. The sooner my son is christened the sooner my mind will rest easy." He took her hand and squeezed her fingers. "Your first godson must have every advantage. And so he shall with you, Alys, and Duncan as godparents."

Duncan looked at Alys in a most particular way and made her feel as if they were alone in the room. His smile began slowly, then broadened to include the others. "My first duty as godfather will be to find the best bottle in your cellars, Ned. Pray excuse me, Miss Champion. And do not fear for my safety. The dragon is in the attic and the Gypsies have disappeared with the darkness." He left her with a reassuring wink.

"What did he mean by that remark?" Giles wondered.

Sommerville glanced at his distant relation and frowned. "What are you waiting for? Away, man! Hurry!" Left alone with Alys, his lordship grabbed her about the waist and swung her round, then set her down and kissed her soundly on the cheek. "A son!"

"After three daughters, did you despair of ever having a boy?" she asked, blushing from his surprising show of emotion.

"Truth to tell, I knew Thea would never fail me. I daresay she gave me three daughters to teach me patience." He looked at her sheepishly and tried to straighten his neckcloth. "Being a father does not come easily to a man of my nature. Perhaps I'll be a better father to my son than I have been to my daughters."

Alys watched him with growing concern. He was so unlike the man she'd always known. These candid revelations were startling and extraordinary. The Viscount Sommerville—a rather starchy gentleman—

simply didn't say such things to his sister-in-law. And his carefree laughter made her suspect that he'd been unhinged by the strain of the last few hours.

Grinning, he rubbed the stubble on his chin. "I dare not present myself to Thea looking like a man half-mad." He yawned. "A little sleep and clean linen will set me to rights. But first I must see that Giles sends word to our nearest and dearest. If he were a little more awake to the world about him, he'd also be sending a nuptial notice to the *Times* and the *Gazette*. But don't despair, Alys. Giles may yet come round. Oh, by the by, tell Duncan we'll uncork the bottle when I'm not so light-headed." He patted her cheek and wandered out like a man drunk with joy.

She sat in a stunned silence. Did Sommerville know of her plans to wed Giles? Were her sentiments so obvious...even to him? For years she'd been circumspect in all her dealings with Giles. What had she done to give away her secret? If everyone else seemed to know, then why didn't Giles?

Briefly, an unthinkable thought entered her head. She began to question her lasting passion for Giles. Firmly she had to remind herself that he was her one true love. Yet quite unexpectedly the doubts had come and, try as she might, she couldn't banish them.

While considering her future with Giles, she wandered over to the window and looked out. The soft light of sunrise began to spread over the horizon. It had been a long, eventful night.

But it wasn't the unpleasant incident in the library that vividly came to her mind. It was the birth of Thea's son. And it was the memory of Duncan's comforting presence…his touch…his kiss that she could not—no, would *never*—forget.

She wondered if instead of a starchy old maid she was more like a brazen hussy. Emma, no doubt, would have much to say concerning her mistress's unladylike behaviour. Alys wondered if it was in the usual way of things for a lady to wed a man who displayed only a tepid affection for her. But what troubled her more was the question of whether a lady should marry one man while having unsettling sentiments for another?

How had her life become an unmanageable mare's nest?

With a tired sigh, she turned from the dawn and started for the door. As she passed the billiard table in the centre of the room, she ran her hand along the cushion rail until her fingertips brushed over the top of a ball. She stared at the ball and picked it up. The gentlemen often played what was known as The Game of Life Pool. She frowned. Was sport truly reflective of life?

"Would you care to play?"

She glanced up and found Duncan standing at the foot of the table, a dusty bottle resting on the rail before him. "You have an exceedingly soft step, sir. Are you stalking me?"

He looked down, hiding the smile that began to tug at the corners of his mouth. "I daresay you, being a lady of excellent perception, would suspect me of such. But truth to tell, I believe you did not hear my approach because of your preoccupation. I've never seen anyone study a ball with such a marked degree of intensity."

"I was pausing for a moment of quiet reflection." She rolled the ball across the table. "Confusion has never before clouded my way. I have always known what I have wanted. And previously, through patience and good management, I've never had any difficulty obtaining a desired result. Yet now..." She gazed at him for a moment, but could not sustain the look he gave her in return. "It must certainly violate the rules of fair play for a sporting gentleman who is instructing a lady in the art of the hunt to poach a kiss from the lady in a manner which robs her of her ability to think clearly." She squared her shoulders and raised her chin, quite determined to continue with her original scheme. For she would not be bested by a sporting man.

"'Tis strange and wondrous, what can be wrought from a meeting of the lips. The time is drawing near when we must see what our scholar can do to clarify your thoughts for you."

She caught herself staring at him in surprise. She hadn't truly thought he would continue with her lessons. "What will you teach me now, sir? How to conduct a dalliance?"

"Regretfully, no," he said, taking a cue stick in his hand. "I fear I must confess to some ungentlemanly behaviour. Earlier, I was outside looking about—for tracks and the like—when you came down to speak to Ned. I watched you—you, Ned *and* Mr. Pomeroy."

"Watching people who don't know you're there is called spying, is it not?"

"In the sporting world it's thought of differently. To slip by an opponent's guard and plant a facer one must be observant. Pugilism and billiards are alike, as they both require looking for the best shot. In pugilism, that means looking for your opponent's weaknesses." He gauged the balance of the cue stick he held. "The game of billiards is also quite a test of skill and judgement. There, too, the able player looks for his best shot. That is what you must learn to do." He moved around to stand next to her. "Would you allow me to demonstrate what I mean?" Without waiting for her assent, he stepped behind her and adjured her to look at the placement of the balls. "What do you see?"

"Several balls scattered about the table. What is it that I ought to see?" She bent down, getting at eye-level with the table.

He leaned over her, his chest brushing her back. His mouth was next to her ear. "A sportsman gains the advantage when he looks for the best shot and can execute his intent.''

The warmth of Duncan's body penetrated the muslin of her morning gown and she shivered.

''Often one must move around the table until the most advantageous approach is found.'' He straightened and led her to the other side of the table. ''From here the placement of the balls seems entirely different, but the balls have not moved. Frequently a player finds his best shot when he changes his position and views the table from another angle. Here, take the sticks and line up your shot. That's it, bend down. Slide the end of the stick over the fingers of your left hand while holding the thick end with your other. Perhaps I should assist you.'' Again he bent over her.

She stiffened.

''Just let me guide you.''

Her hands began to moisten and her throat became parched. She stood abruptly, scraping his chin with her shoulder. ''I believe this lesson must wait for another day. I cannot concentrate on the ball and my hand trembles. No doubt I am fatigued.'' She backed away from him. In her retreat she nearly knocked the bottle off the end of the rail.

He smiled. ''No doubt you wish to retire.''

Clutching the neck of the bottle, she said, ''Sommerville has already gone up. He said that your toast would have to wait.''

His smile softened. "Does not anticipation heighten the moment of realization?"

Her cheeks warmed at the thoughts his words engendered. Was he intent upon kissing her again? Without knowing quite what she was doing, she raised her hand and brushed her fingers over her lips. She gasped and stared at him before hastening her retreat from the antechamber.

Stroking his chin, Duncan watched her flee. "Hie away, vixen . . . for the chase is on." Smiling to himself, he murmured, "Tally-ho."

CHAPTER NINE

AT NOON, after a few hours of dream-filled sleep, Alys tiptoed into her sister's bedchamber. The drapes had been drawn nearly closed to exclude most of the sunlight. Yet even though the room was deeply shadowed, Alys could appreciate its recently refurbished appearance. It had been done up for the guests the new mother was expected to receive after her confinement.

Moving to the Grecian bed, hung with fringed silk, Alys looked down at Thea and saw that her sister still slept. The likelihood of her waking very soon was not worth reckoning. Who would begrudge her the hours of recuperative rest?

She began to withdraw quietly when a sound from the far side of the bed stayed her. Sommerville leaned out from the shadow of the silk hangings and smiled sheepishly at her. He tapped a finger to his lips, then gazed at her enquiringly.

His vigil obviously was not meant to be revealed. It mattered not that she thought there were far too many secrets between Thea and her husband. She supposed she would have to honour his request, and she nodded her assent.

Giving a relieved sigh, he gently took Thea's hand in his as he sat down on a nearby chair to watch her sleep.

Not wanting to intrude upon his private moment, Alys backed away, exiting through the dressing-room. She paused in the doorway, surprised to find the room occupied.

There sat the wet nurse, with bodice strings undone and a foul-smelling liquid dribbling down her chin. The woman tried to hide the gin bottle, but only managed to slosh its contents down the side of her skirt.

Alys firmly closed the door and advanced into the chamber. "How dare you! How dare you partake of strong drink while suckling the young heir." Her ire began to build, for it was well known that a baby took on the character of the one who suckled him.

"Oh, pleez mizz!" the woman wailed. "Don't be tellin' her ladyship."

"Hush! Lower your voice. I don't want my sister awakened by your caterwauling." Alys restrained herself from shaking the woman. "Have you no thought for the child?"

"That I do! I was juz' dosin' meself against all the disease that's in th' village...and this house. You wouldn't be wanting me to take the grippe like the nanny, now would you?" The wet nurse picked up her bottle and wiped the mouth of it, then offered it to Alys. "Here, you be needin' a bit of the spirits yo'r-self." She hiccupped. "M' dad took a regular dose of gin every day of his life and was never sick. O' course, he died after fallin' in the well one night. But he was never sick, on that I swear."

Controlling the rise of her temper, Alys stalked past the woman and peered into the baby's cradle, which was by the small fireplace. She prayed that his peaceful slumbers owed nothing to gin. "Why aren't you and the infant boy upstairs where you belong? His lordship will be most displeased if you disturb his lady."

"The old woman with the dog—" the wet nurse paused to lick the gin from her chin "—said I was to stay down here. Dr. Wingate fears that the nanny's sickness might be catchin'."

Gazing at the slovenly woman, Alys wondered who had hired her and where a replacement could be found. With illness in the village and also at Green Hill House, she doubted a suitable woman could be hired who'd be willing to risk contracting an ailment.

"Clean yourself up," she said crisply to the woman. "And no more gin, not while you suckle the babe." She grabbed the bottle.

The woman wailed, pleading vociferously for her bottle of spirits. "It's the only thing that'll save me from the plague!"

"The grippe is not the plague. Besides, if I catch you imbibing strong spirits again you'll wish the plague would indeed carry you away." At the woman's teary look of incomprehension Alys stated, "Drink gin while in this house and you'll be turned away without a farthing. Do you understand me now?"

The wet nurse nodded, but buried her head in her apron and continued to bawl.

"If you must cry," Alys said, resigned to the woman's carryings-on, "do so quietly. Her ladyship is sleeping."

Lord Sommerville stepped into the room, looking cross and bewildered. "Woman, be silent! Alys, what's the meaning of this?" he asked at last, when the wet nurse subsided into noisy sniffles. "This sort of commotion is bound to wake Thea."

And, indeed, from the next room, the new mother was calling to them both. Alys cast Sommerville an apologetic look, before hurrying to answer the summons.

"I'll be along in a moment," he said, gazing over at the cradle. His voice softened as he said, "As soon as I've had a good look at him."

In the bedchamber, Alys rang for the maid, helped her sister to sit up, fluffed her pillows, and begged pardon for disturbing her sleep.

Thea sighed tiredly as she sank back into her bed. "There's no need to blame yourself. What would we do without you? My mind is at peace knowing you are in charge.'' She stretched, then pulled at the bands that bound her chest. ''These things are the very devil. But a necessary evil, I suppose. Would you be so kind as to fetch my brush from the dressing-table? I wouldn't want Sommerville to see me in such a sad state.''

''I'm afraid he's already seen you in disarray. He—''

''I looked in on you a moment ago,'' Sommerville interposed as he came back into the room. He gave Alys a quelling glance before resuming his place at the bedside.

With growing anticipation, Alys waited for them to speak the words of love they'd each declared to her only hours before. But nothing came.

Thea glanced at her husband, then lowered her lashes and blushed when his warm gaze remained overlong on her. Sommerville, for his part, lapsed into diplomatic silence.

Sorely tempted to take matters into her own hands, Alys struggled to resist her natural inclination to set matters right. She could reveal what each had said to her, but felt she would be breaking the trust they'd placed in her. Besides, Thea deserved to hear Sommerville's words of love from his own lips.

Had the passage of time sealed the words in his heart? In the throes of worry, when he had thought Thea might die, he'd expressed himself without restraint. She wondered what could now cause him to be as forthcoming. And what could she do to help things along?

Perhaps they only needed the right opportunity. Sommerville would not likely utter the desired words before an audience, no matter how small. They needed time alone.

"You must excuse me," Alys said, sidling towards the door, "but the cook needs to be taken to task for last night's repast. The beef was dry and the asparagus soup..." She grimaced, then smiled at Thea. "I shall speak to him on your behalf, dearest. You needn't worry about your household. I shall see that all runs smoothly. Rest now." She slipped out before either could utter a word to stay her.

The first footman she happened upon was sent to the schoolroom to inform Emma, who was presently in charge of the girls, that Nanny Jinks was to be confined to a room far removed from her charges. Another footman was sent to fetch Dr. Wingate. Alys then summoned the butler and instructed him to assemble the servants. In no time Alys was addressing them.

"Lady Sommerville is kind-hearted," she stated, as she began to move along the line of minions, from the haughty butler to the lowly scullery maid. "You have taken advantage of her good nature. For years this household has been ruled from below stairs. I have assumed, for a time, my sister's duties as mistress of this house and I shall regain for her the management of it. I daresay if I reckoned the accounts someone would be turned away without a character.'' The butler blustered and pulled on his collar. She chose to ignore him, for the time being. ''Under my direction this establishment shall become a well-run residence. We shall begin in the kitchen. I daresay the inmates at Newgate have fare more edible than what we've sampled this week.''

As the cook sputtered, Alys went on to issue her orders. By the time she was finished there were several disgruntled servants among those who filed out, muttering mutinously.

Alys knew that she had razed the structure that had existed below stairs. But for some inexplicable reason she desired to take the hard way in this. She wanted something that would so occupy her mind that she would have no time for thought. She needed to lose herself in her duties, but she was reluctant to examine her need too closely.

Later that afternoon, after hours spent at her many duties, she paced impatiently in the entrance hall, counting the squares of chequered marble on the floor. By busying her mind with this trivial pastime she hoped to divert her thoughts from certain pressing matters which could not be dealt with at the moment.

She glanced at the tall case clock, then frowned. Would the doctor never come? Did he intend to sleep away the entire day?

As she kept her vigil, she heard a thud on the stairs. Descending at a slow rate, Giles came down one step at a time. Before his nose he held a sheaf of papers, the examination of which occupied his whole attention. He brushed past Alys as if she weren't there.

"Good afternoon, sir," she said distinctly.

He jerked round as if someone had sprung at him from a dark recess. "Miss Champion, you must not startle a man as he exercises his mind." He frowned, his thick brows drawing together. "You've chased my thoughts clear away, and I was contemplating a most important matter. I can see where your nieces get their high spirits. I'd not thought that the ladies of your family were such an unsettled lot."

She decided to look for her best shot. "After my sisters married they led the most placid of lives. I daresay it will be the same when I wed."

"Then I advise you not to delay any longer."

Feigning a look of bashful innocence, she said, "La, sir. You mustn't tease me so, for you know as well as I that a lady must await an offer before she can wed."

Giles brows shot up, making his stunned look complete. "Do you mean you've not been asked...not once during all these years? Are you of a sickly disposition, Miss Champion?"

"I enjoy vigorous health, sir." Perhaps she needed to drop a broader hint. "My heart is set on marrying for love. And I admire greatly a man whose mind is keen and whose soul is dedicated to good.''

''I hesitate to defame the fellow, Miss Champion, but he must be a slowtop. How sharp-witted can he be if he hasn't deduced your delicate sentiments? Mind you, a man of intellect doesn't hold with these fanciful female emotions. To a man of science love is a will-o'-the-wisp. I, myself, do not believe in the mystical or the magical. A subject must be proven true before I will embrace it.'' He rapped his papers with his hand. ''Here is Truth, and she demands my all. Pardon, but I have no time for prattle. My work awaits me.''

She stared after him. Could she ever convince him of the reality of love—an emotion, an intangible condition of the heart?

With a growing sense of disquiet, she sighed. How odd, that she didn't feel Giles's rejection more keenly. The thought that it would be necessary to consult with Duncan Todd about this newest development filled her with foreboding.

She had successfully avoided him all day, having decided that if she couldn't manage him when they were alone, then they would never again be alone. Thus her numerous duties had kept her occupied and in the company of others.

Reluctantly, though, she came to the conclusion that sooner or later she would have to approach Duncan for a private conversation. She wondered what he, an expert in the art of the hunt, would make of Giles's belief that love did not exist.

Fortunately, she was able to push all her personal concerns aside when at last Dr. Wingate arrived. She hurried him upstairs, hardly allowing him time to shrug out of his greatcoat. He obviously disliked being rushed, for he protested every step of the way.

Alys stopped before Thea's bedchamber door and held the doctor back from entering. "Prepare yourself, sir. You may not be best pleased with the decisions which, of necessity, have been made." She rapped on the door, then stepped aside as she went in and motioned for the doctor to follow her. Voices came from behind a dressing screen.

Old Peony emerged from the screen carrying a bundle of wrapping bands. "Daresay you feel a mite better now, your ladyship. Nothin' like that feelin' of bein' freed. The milk will come soon enough, never you fear."

"What is the meaning of this?" Dr. Wingate demanded, pushing past Alys and hurrying towards the screen.

Catching him before he crossed the room, Alys whispered, "The wet nurse is wholly unsuitable. Unusual measures had to be taken. Her ladyship has agreed to suckle the young heir herself."

"This is your doing," he hissed, looking quite livid. "I shall speak to her ladyship. 'Tis folly to pursue the course you've set for her. Plain folly." He cleared his throat and asked, "Your ladyship, might I approach and speak to you privately... as doctor to patient?"

Thea came out from behind the screen, fastening a dressing-gown about her, and slipped back into bed. She beckoned the doctor to a chair. They began conversing in quiet voices.

"How fares the babe?" Alys asked the midwife.

Old Peony sighed and clasped her hands over her rounded middle. "He does well enough. That tosspot they had to hire as a wet nurse won't likely wake until nightfall. She's no fit nurse for the heir." She snorted and returned to her duties.

While the midwife folded the wrapping bands, Alys listened to the drone of Dr. Wingate's voice. After a few minutes his tone changed from cajoling to declaring, from declaring to pleading, then, apparently as a last resort, he used his voice of doom.

"Alys," Thea called when at last the doctor ended his harangue, "please come here. Dr. Wingate wishes to speak to us both."

Alys sat on the edge of the bed and gave her attention to the physician.

He authoritatively clasped the facings of his coat and frowned, burying his chin into his neck. "Forgive the directness that I am now forced to use." He cleared his throat. "It is a grave mistake for a lady of Quality to suckle her child. In my generation it was considered quite indelicate for a lady to do so. I have observed that gently bred females haven't the required sufficiency of anatomy to completely fulfil the needs of the child. Those ladies who were unwise enough to have undertaken this hazardous course discovered that their upper portions increased to an unseemly roundness. We must remember that there is the very real danger of forever altering her ladyship's figure."

"It was altered long ago with the birth of my first child," Thea remarked, running a hand over her middle.

Alys looked at the doctor politely. "Sir, are you advising that we allow the young heir to be tended by a—a sot?" She eyed him suspiciously. "Who hired this woman as wet nurse?"

"I regret the necessity which compelled me to seek her services . . . that is, ah . . ." He reddened and stammered to a halt. Gathering his dignity, he cleared his throat and said, "I shall speak to his lordship . . . and the dowager will hear of this."

"You must do as you think right," Thea said. "But I tell you, sir, that as the welfare of my son is my prime concern I shall do what I think best. I will suckle him myself."

Alys smiled at her sister, surprised by her determination. She wondered if Thea could face the dowager with this same courage and poise. She would know soon enough, for Sommerville's mother and the rest of their kith and kin would be arriving for the christening on Sunday next.

"I will sleep now," Thea stated. "Old Peony tells me that rest and nourishment are what a nursing mother needs most." She closed her eyes, obviously dismissing them.

The doctor muttered all the way to the door. "Meddling ... officious ... impertinent ... old maid," he said under his breath. With a curt nod and a glare, he left Alys. He tossed a threat over his shoulder as he went. "His lordship shall hear of this!"

CHAPTER TEN

A FEW EVENINGS LATER, Duncan and Sommerville sat at their ease in the Great Room, the only place they could find to have a quiet word together. Their chairs were drawn up before the fireplace and an old bottle of Madeira rested on a table between them.

Sommerville stared into the amber-coloured wine and swirled it slowly about in the glass. "Dr. Wingate tells me that my wife's health is weakening due to the demands of the baby. Thea says he speaks a lot of nonsense. Yet she does sleep more than she ever had before, though when she's awake she seems to be flourishing— She's radiant, actually."

"Motherhood brings with it a certain charm," Duncan commented.

"Thea's never looked more beautiful." Sommerville stared at the fire, then swallowed his wine in one gulp. "I should tell her." He rapped the arm of his chair. "Ha! What I should do is tell her sister to stop looking at me so expectantly."

"What does she expect you to do?"

"She doesn't say. She just looks at me as if she's waiting for me to do something momentous." Sommerville scowled. "On the night that Thea delivered our son, I was in a sad state. I feared that Thea wouldn't survive her travail. Alys happened to come down at my weakest moment and she became the recipient of some very personal disclosures. It was odd that I could tell her things I would never utter in the presence of another man. I daresay Alys is waiting for me to say those same things to Thea."

Duncan smiled to himself. Yes, of course, that spirited lady would want her sister's happiness to come before her own. Evidently she was determined that Sommerville should declare his sentiments. Well, why not?

Turning so that he might scrutinize his host, Duncan said in surprised tones, "Ned, do you mean to say you have never spoken to your wife of your sentiments?"

Sommerville hemmed and hawed before answering. "It seems improper for a gentleman to speak to his wife of passion. If you were married, you'd know what I mean."

"My father is considered a very proper gentleman. On numerous occasions he has been overheard to declare his sentiments to my mother. I've even seen him many times with his arm about her waist. Of course he's never made a cake of himself in public, but I *know* how my father feels towards my mother."

"I wonder if I should...." Sommerville gazed at the flames in the grate.

Duncan kept silent for a time, letting his crony come to his own conclusions. Besides, who was he to tell another man how to win his lady? For days, Alys had been like a fox gone to ground. She avoided all conversations with him, even though she appeared to have something she wished to discuss. And, unless there was another adult present, she refused to stay in the same room.

His only comfort came from knowing that her progress with Pomeroy had come to a standstill. He knew he needed to seize the advantage and find a way to have a private word with Alys.

Though preoccupied with his contemplations, Duncan dimly perceived a growing commotion out in the hall.

When at last the noise reached a level that could no longer be ignored, Sommerville looked at the door with foreboding. "Blast! What is it now? What new disaster has befallen us?"

Dr. Wingate threw open the door and stood seething in the entrance. "Sir, your sister-in-law is an impossible female!"

Sommerville turned to Duncan, his countenance revealing the sentiments of a man pressed to his limits. "What is it this time, Doctor?"

"As her ladyship is suffering from some odd humours," the doctor said, coming up to the fire and warming his hands, "I deemed it advisable to cup her. Miss Champion, a spinster of outlandish and varied opinions, interfered with the practise of the healing art. She flatly refused me access to my patient."

"Ah, she did?"

Duncan detected the sound of relief in Sommerville's voice.

"My lord, if I am to continue as her ladyship's physician, then I must have no opposition. I will not have my judgement questioned!"

Sommerville bowed his head in a thoughtful attitude. "I appreciate your dilemma, Doctor. I hope you appreciate mine. Her ladyship trusts her sister implicitly. My wife's judgement is acceptable to me." He glanced up, a hard look in his eyes. "Is it acceptable to you?"

Pulling on his neckcloth, Dr. Wingate nodded vigorously. "Of—of course! I never meant . . . It shall be as your lordship desires."

As the doctor withdrew, a group of servants, led by the butler, slipped into the room. The cook and her ladyship's dresser were among the throng.

"Yes?" Sommerville said, not looking at all pleased by the intrusion.

"M'lord," said the butler, who stepped forward as the spokesman and bowed, "pardon our presumption—"

Sommerville held up his hand. "Does this . . . ah, committee have something to say concerning my lady's sister?"

"Yes, m'lord. May I speak freely?" The butler assumed his most haughty posture.

Giving a sigh of forbearance, Sommerville said, "This is England. Speak your piece."

Though given permission, the butler hesitated until Lady Sommerville's dresser prodded him from behind. "M'lord," he said, "we, your humble servants, have enjoyed rendering many years of service to you and her ladyship. Lady Sommerville's goodness and sweet-tempered manner are well known. Her kindness makes our labours seem light. But gentle ways are not always shared in a family."

Sommerville, who'd been listening with his head bowed, looked up and leaned back in his chair.

"There is one in this house," the butler continued, "who would change the order of things. This new mistress wishes to set aside the established methods. We all feel her trespass. Even Nanny Jinks, who remains ill, grows increasingly distressed by the laxity in the schoolroom. The smooth working of the household is in danger of coming to a halt."

Duncan watched his friend close his eyes and rub his forehead, an indication of the resurgence of his ire.

"I see," Sommerville murmured, clearly keeping a rein on his temper. "Each of you agrees that this house was run before in a smooth fashion? Each of you agrees that your mistress's deputy has meddled beyond the bounds of her authority?" He looked at them individually. "Is this correct?"

In accord, they clamoured their agreement.

For a moment Sommerville seemed caught up in his own thoughts. Then he looked at the butler and said, "Very well, ask Miss Champion if she would attend me here." While the servants filed out, he poured himself another glass of wine.

"I daresay you will want to conduct your interview in private," Duncan said, rising from his chair.

Sommerville stared at him with astonishment. "How did you come by that addle-pated notion? A man would have to be either marvellously heroic or hopelessly stupid to face my sister-in-law alone. She's cunning. And she uses logic." He drank deeply of the wine. "It's deuced unfair of a woman to use logic—throws a man off his stride."

"A man known for his diplomacy should be able to gain the advantage handily. Ned, you needn't dread this opportunity. Leave off looking like a cock about to have his neck wrung. She can hardly feast on your carcass."

"Strong-willed females have ever been my downfall." Shamefaced, he looked away. "In the past I've steered clear of them. The dowager is just such a one. Since my father's death, she's become more pugnacious with the passing of each year. Dashed unpleasant to be around." Apparently Ned had even ceased to refer to his mother in familiar terms.

Duncan could not envision his friend flinching from anyone, not after having seen him square off willy-nilly with the brawniest that Jackson's had to offer. "Don't think of Miss Champion as your sister-in-law. Think of her as a bruiser in the ring."

"I do not spar with ladies."

"Of course not. But in a verbal sense you must be ready to take a few jabs from her, and, in turn, be prepared to present your best effort, in defence and offence. When all is said and done, the worst she can do is box your ears."

Sommerville gave him a doubtful look.

Taking a stance before the fireplace, Duncan tried to bolster him with an encouraging smile. "No one knows what he can do till he tries. Have you tried?" He watched as Sommerville's mouth slowly set into a firm line, and his eyes narrowed and grew steely. "Remain resolute, Ned. Here she comes."

Alys entered with the briskness of someone who'd been called away from a demanding occupation. "Yes, Sommerville? What is it you wished to say to me? It must be quite important, for you must know that I was taking an inventory of the linens."

"You mustn't do so much." Sommerville nearly reached for his glass of wine, but instead he clasped his hands and cleared his throat. "That, in essence, is what I wished to speak to you about."

Duncan moved away from the fireplace, motioning for Sommerville to take his place, then he went to a window embrasure and looked out. He wanted to distance himself from what was about to transpire. The success or failure of the interview now rested on the shoulders of his friend.

From his commanding position before the fire, Sommerville motioned for Alys to be seated. After hesitating a moment, she complied. "It has come to my attention," he said, clasping his hands behind his back, "that my household is on the verge of collapse. There are matters which need to be addressed immediately."

Alys nodded her agreement. "The schoolroom does need to be refurbished. It's much too bleak. Of course, for the best results you might begin by turning away Nanny Jinks. She hasn't an ounce of kindness in her; I've yet to meet a more dour woman. It seems logical that if one wants pleasant children one should hire a pleasant nursery maid."

Duncan ignored Sommerville's covert, beseeching glance. "The nursery isn't what I was referring to when I spoke of my household collapsing," his lordship said, giving her a serious look. "There's been a mismanagement of domestic affairs."

"Oh, I see," she replied, smiling archly at him. "Well, sir, if you think you can persuade me to mend the rift between you and Thea, you are much mistaken. My sister deserves a husband who will do his own wooing. You may have mismanaged the affair for years, but, with a little effort, you may yet redeem yourself."

He glared at her, appearing quite surly. "My marriage is not on the verge of collapse. It's the dashed awful state of affairs in the servants' quarters that I wanted to speak to you about—not about my children, and certainly not about my wife!" He picked up his glass of wine and swallowed the Madeira, apparently wanting to cool his temper with it. "The servants are in an uproar. One wonders if there will be food on the board in the morning."

Alys sat forward. "It gladdens my heart that you are taking an interest in what has come to pass below stairs. I've been wanting to speak to you on just this matter. I wouldn't dare trouble Thea with it." Her expression turned to one of annoyance. " 'Insurrection' best describes it. I've never witnessed such a want of decorum in servants. If they were mine—"

"That is just the point," Sommerville stated. "They are not *your* servants. As Thea's deputy, you are doing a great service for us both. You have a great deal of confidence. You were born to lead." He frowned and looked at her squarely. "But your service as mistress of the house will come to an end. I do not mean to sound ungrateful, but I must ask you this: if *you* bring the servants to order, how will Thea regain their loyalty and respect? Granted, she's struggled against great odds before now. But would she ever succeed in reaching the mark of your legacy?"

Alys's gaze fell before his. She remained thoughtfully silent for a moment. "Forgive me. I hadn't meant to displace Thea or encroach upon her authority. I merely saw a state of affairs which needed attention." She glanced up at Sommerville, giving him a tight, crooked smile. "Your servants *are* a pack of indolent connivers."

"A worse lot of ne'er-do-wells I've yet to see," he said in agreement. "The dowager gave them to us. I have often wondered if she was attempting to show her disapproval of our marriage. But in the end she'll not best us. Thea will come about and take her proper place as Viscountess Sommerville."

She gazed at her brother-in-law for a long moment. "How curious. I've never seen you look so assured and resolute." With a bemused expression, she glanced over at Duncan. "There are some inexplicable transformations taking place in this house, and I've not had a hand in them. I wonder who..."

Duncan met her gaze. He felt no guilt of chicanery. His aim was not to change people, but to help them find the fine qualities they already possessed, yet had misplaced. The strength of a man wasn't in the bravado he showed the world, but in the depth of the wellspring he could draw upon.

"Ned, if you have no objection," Duncan said abruptly, "I'll see Miss Champion to her room, since the hour is late and she has obviously had a long day."

Taking her hand, Sommerville clasped it warmly. "Alys, I pray I haven't offended you. Both Thea and I cherish you for your goodness of heart and willingness to help wherever and whenever you're needed." Giving her a grateful smile, he handed her over to Duncan.

When the library door closed behind them, Alys slumped against it, leaning her head upon Duncan's shoulder. After a moment he tipped up her chin and was surprised to find tears in her eyes.

"Pardon me. I hardly ever cry," she said with a defiant sniff. "It's only that I realize I have indeed become a meddling old ape leader. Before, I had called myself one only as a jest. Yet now it actually applies.''

''Does it? You don't look very old.''

''I am twenty-seven,'' she retorted. ''I have lingered for years on the shelf.''

He patted her hand solicitously as he led her to the marble staircase, then they began their ascent. ''At five-and-thirty, I've lingered a mite longer than you, and no one yet considers me long in the tooth.''

''With men age is a distinction. To ladies it's a plague.'' Sighing, she shook her head, as if baffled by the lack of fairness in life. ''No one comments if a man weds at the age of thirty. Yet if a woman does, she is considered blessed beyond measure and quite lucky to have found someone to take her off her family's hands.''

''None the less, ape leader is much too harsh a term for a loving aunt.''

''But I *am* meddlesome,'' she said in a forlorn voice. ''I have become too managing—offensively so.''

''Abhorrently so,'' he added with a twinkle. He decided it was time to put a stop to her self-censure. ''You must reform. Of late, you have been much too busy. These last days you have hardly stopped long enough in your housekeeping to take the air. What you need is a pleasure outing. It will put the colour back in your cheeks.'' He stopped before the door to her chamber. ''Tomorrow promises to be a fine day. You and I shall take leave of our duties in the afternoon.''

She looked at him suspiciously. "What shall we do?"

Smiling at her kindly, he opened her door and, with his hand on her back, guided her into the room. "We shall fish." He closed the door on any protest she might utter.

ALYS GAZED OUT over the sunlit terrace. Indeed it was a fine day. And what harm could come of fishing from the embankment at the lawn's edge in full view of the house?

A light breeze played with the ribbons of her chip hat. She smoothed the jonquil muslin of her walking dress and set the collar of her dark blue spencer. Looking down at her attire, she wondered if she were suitably garbed for an afternoon of fishing.

She didn't care to question what vanity had prompted her to don her best and try to present a pleasing appearance. Nor had she an answer to why, after days of avoiding him, she was going fishing with Duncan. The day was much too fine for what was sure to be a vexing examination of her soul.

As she enjoyed the beauty of the view, she beheld Duncan, hatless and in top-boots, walking up towards her from the river. His long, even strides had a manly grace which captured her notice. In no time, he effortlessly closed the distance between them. She could see by his countenance that the outdoors was indeed his domain.

With a slow survey, he took in her apparel and smiled. "How fetching you look, Miss Champion." He bowed formally before her. His close-cropped raven hair glistened in the sunlight, tempting her to reach out and feel its texture.

"Won't you be needing your hat?" she asked, hoping to put temptation out of sight.

Chuckling, he straightened. "I have lost far too many when faced with the choice of holding on to a fish or to my hat." He offered his arm. "If you're quite ready, shall we go?"

They strolled companionably over the lawn, making observations on the pleasant weather. Down at the water's edge, Alys looked about, wondering from what spot they would fish. She thought it odd that she couldn't see any sign of rods, creel or angling net awaiting them. The only thing in sight was a row-boat moored next to the low embankment.

Duncan moved along the bank and stopped before the boat, which contained all the equipment they would need. He slipped into it, keeping his balance when it tipped slightly. He got his footing, then reached up, ready to receive her.

Looking at him doubtfully, Alys hesitated. She was more wary of the water than the boat. With a sweep of her arm, she indicated the length of the embankment. "Shan't we avail ourselves of this lovely spot? It's so convenient . . . within sight of the house."

His eyes gleamed wickedly as he gazed up at her. "Is that the opinion of an ape leader, or a spirited woman who is ripe for an adventure?'' Again he held up his arms.

Willy-nilly she placed her hands on his shoulders and allowed him to ease her into the boat. As the craft dipped, he clasped her about the waist and drew her near to him. The motion beneath them settled into subtle, rhythmic rocking.

Not quite trusting the caprice of the boat, she clung to him. For a moment it seemed as if the swaying of the craft were the cause of her unsteadiness. Then, as the seconds passed, she discovered that the perturbation within her could only be attributed to Duncan's body pressed close to hers.

She strove to compose herself. But her disquiet continued until she stepped out of his arms and sat down to regain her self-command. ''The day seems to be turning warmer,'' she said, pressing a hand to her heated cheek.

''But not as warm as it could be,'' he countered. His gaze rested upon her for an uncomfortably long time before he released the lines and pushed away from the embankment. After placing the oars in the water, he began to row with smooth, strong strokes.

''Where are you taking us?'' she asked, gazing about. She tried to avoid looking at the appealing sight he made as he fluidly manoeuvred the oars.

He laid into his labour, propelling them upstream with each mighty pull. ''We're making for the point just off Eel Pie Island. 'Tis not very far. There we will find an old mooring stone we can put to use.''

"It sounds secluded. Are you quite sure that it is fishing you are intent upon, or is it some other sport?" She folded her hands primly on her lap. Would he try to teach her some new aspect of the hunt? "Is this an instructive expedition of an amatory nature?"

He let the boat drift for a moment as he regarded her over the oars. "Are you thinking that I'll attempt to seduce you? In a row-boat?" he added with a hint of a chuckle. "I daresay every boatman on the Thames would find that most entertaining indeed."

Disconcerted, she glanced away. If she cared to look deeply within herself—and she didn't—she knew she would find that it was her desires she distrusted, more than his. Though she seemed to struggle with it daily, she could not manage to erase the memory of his kiss. It lingered, taunting her, and his image wouldn't leave her in peace.

When they'd first met, she had not found his sort of handsomeness appealing. The brooding, poetic thinker had always attracted her more than the swarthy, rugged man who preferred the outdoors. But now she found that a pair of capable, strong hands and a set of broad, muscled shoulders were the finest of God's creations. She experienced great disquiet as recollections of his blue eyes, his dark hair and his firm mouth haunted her day and night.

She wondered if she were losing her senses; to be so possessed seemed most odd. A lady of sound judgement surely would not allow herself to be swayed by the physical attributes of a gentleman.

If only he weren't so kind and noble. Her former bias had allowed her to think comfortably of sporting men as boorish oafs, but, since meeting Duncan, she'd come to see that she'd been unjust. There was more to him than his love of sport.

He was all that a gentleman should be: gentle but manly, considerate but not condescending. He was— She refused to allow herself to go on. To admit that he was the sort of man who might make her happy would be a betrayal of her long-cherished illusions.

Glancing up, she found him watching her. A singular glow in his eyes slowly warmed her to the very core of her soul. Without warning, she sensed that that part of herself she'd always held in reserve was giving way. Her last defence seemed to crumble before his fervid regard, and she felt exposed.

Without a pause, as if aware of her vulnerability, he silently rowed on until the shore of Eel Pie Island loomed behind him. After gently drifting to the mooring stone, he raised the oars and then secured the line. He handed her a rod and gallantly baited the hook for her, then dropped it down into the water.

"Angling is said to rest the mind," Duncan remarked as if to himself, "cheer the spirit, divert sadness, and calm unquiet thoughts. It is a moderator of passions, a procurer of contentedness, it begets habits of peace and patience." Apparently forsaking these benefits himself, he reclined against the bow and seemed to wait for her to speak. After a time, as the silence became prolonged, his eyes closed.

Alys bit her lip and looked down at the water. How could she put her feelings into words? Besides, she didn't trust the sudden revelation of her sentiments. She needed time to examine and test them. It simply wasn't logical that, after eight years of devotion, she could forsake Giles in favour of Duncan, a man she'd known for less than a fortnight.

Resting her elbow on the boat's gunwale and her chin on her fist, she idly held the rod as she stared deeper into the depths of the river. In her mind she struggled to comprehend what was happening to her. She could understand her admiration for Duncan; he was a fine man with many splendid qualities.

She couldn't help wondering if her father might also have possessed some of these qualities. She tried to picture him as a young man. Her mother wouldn't have married a boorish fellow with no goodness of nature. Whatever had occurred between her parents to drive them into their own worlds, she was sure that they had once shared tender sentiments. She clutched the side of the boat, feeling a great wave of remorse for having judged her father so harshly for far too long.

She might never have gained this insight had Duncan not helped her to view things differently. It was like walking round the billiard table and seeing the arrangement of the balls from a new perspective.

Bit by tiny bit, her disposition had begun to alter. There was still a long road to be travelled, but he'd pointed the way. There had been no coercion. She'd taken to the path on her own.

Duncan possessed that certain degree of trust in his fellowmen that gave him the confidence to let them strike out on their own. And he held that same trust in womankind. Alys had never sensed that he thought her an inferior being, or viewed ladies as creatures needing a keeper.

But he was also the sort of man who wouldn't allow a female to take control of his life. His course was set, and the woman who became his wife would be a helpmate, not the manager of his affairs.

She doubted that she would be the sort of lady he would choose to wed and the thought saddened her.

As he reposed, she gazed at him. She hadn't realized that his dark lashes were so long. He was indeed handsome, for his strength of character was set in each feature.

The planes of his face teased her to touch them. She wished that instead of a rod she might cradle his head on her lap.

It was then that she noticed the tautness of the line and the pull on the rod as it slipped through her fingers. Taken by surprise, she awkwardly grabbed the pole. She stood and, bracing one foot against the side of the boat, yanked on it. The boat lurched precariously.

The fish, a great fighter, jerked the line this way and that. Then it skimmed the surface and plunged into the river's depths.

She was pulled until she leant half out of the boat. "Duncan!" As she cried out the boat tipped, dipped and cast her over the side.

She swallowed a little water as she went under. The ribbons of her hat nearly strangled her until she tore it off. Struggling to emerge, she wished she truly knew how to swim. *God give me strength,* she prayed.

The cold water was a chilling hand pulling her down. She fought to reach the surface and finally did so. Gulping air, she flailed for a moment before beginning to sink again.

She kicked her legs, but her clinging skirts hampered the effort. Her face went under and she tried once more to regain the surface. Yet she could feel the river pulling the strength from her.

As she sank deeper, she regretted that she would never again feel Duncan's arms about her. With one last effort she surged for the light at the top, knowing she couldn't hold her breath any longer.

From somewhere above a hand clasped hers, an arm caught her about the waist and she was pulled upward.

As she broke the surface, she gasped for air.

"Thank God! I thought Old Grim had got you." Duncan cried, clasping her to him as he treaded water.

STILL DAMP and clutching Duncan's coat, Alys leaned against him as she mounted the marble stairs at Green Hill House. The river scent, redolent of fish, lingered with them. She swept her wet hair back and managed to ascend one more step. Her walking dress stuck to her, hampering her natural stride.

Her modesty had been left at the river's edge when, with clinging muslin defining her every curve, Duncan had insisted that he carry her across the lawn. The servants had stared as the pair entered the house, and they were still staring. Alys couldn't blame them for their pop-eyed looks. Duncan cut a rather dashing figure in his wet shirt and breeches. And as for the revelation of her form...well, Duncan's coat failed to cover her sufficiently.

Emma hurried down to meet her with a blanket. Exclaiming and scolding, the maid cast aside the dripping coat and wrapped the blanket about Alys.

Glancing to the top of the stairs, Alys saw Giles gaping at her, dumbfounded. She noticed his gaze was fixed on her lower limbs, where the damp muslin revealed much of her leg as she climbed the steps.

His peeping infuriated her, and she glared at him, her temper steadily rising. What sort of gentleman would gape so vulgarly at a woman when she was clearly at a disadvantage? Had Giles no true sense of honour?

"Were you caught in a downpour?" Giles asked, finally tearing his eyes from her limbs. "I believe the day has been mostly sunny. How odd that you should return soaked to the skin." His gaze again ran the length of Alys.

Stepping before her, Duncan confronted the scholar. "There's a relic downstairs which demands your attention. Go and feast your eyes upon *it*. The lady has no need for your pointed regard."

Surprisingly, Giles stood his ground. "By what right do you presume to speak for Miss Champion?"

"Mr. Todd saved my life," Alys said.

"Oh, Miss Alys, how very exciting," Emma exclaimed.

"That still doesn't give this farmer the authority to speak on her behalf." Giles retreated a step, backing out of arm's reach. "But I do have important work to do. Miss Champion, I hope you will leg— I mean, let me call on you later to see how you fare. Ahh..." He inhaled deeply. "We must be having fish for dinner. How tasty!" He hastened away.

Alys sneezed, and felt chilled to the bone.

"Put her in a hot bath," Duncan said to Emma, "and see that she rests without intrusion." He took Alys by the hand. "I see I have been remiss in my instruction. I shall have to teach you how to swim."

With a surge of her old spirit, Alys asked, "Is that an art of the hunt?"

His smile seemed to be self-mocking as he smoothed back a wet strand of her hair. "Obviously we've stumbled upon the bait that will lure Mr. Pomeroy to the altar."

Alys wanted to retort, but instead she battled the onslaught of a sneeze.

"Come along, Miss Alys," Emma said, leading her away. "The maids are preparing the bath in her ladyship's dressing-room."

A short while later, immersed in steaming water, Alys found contentment and peace. She leant back and basked in the warmth of the water and the fire that burned in the nearby grate. The door leading into Thea's bedchamber stood ajar.

Alys heard her sister softly singing a lullaby. Sitting forward and peering into the next room, she glimpsed Thea holding the babe to her breast and smiling tenderly.

How odd it felt to envy Thea her good fortune. Alys had always pitied her sister for her lack of courage and strength of character; yet, seeing Thea with her child brought a new insight. Though her older sister possessed the gentle qualities of a peacemaker, there was a power in her that blossomed when familial or maternal demands called.

Her sister's life held boundless promise, but Alys saw a future of uncertainty for herself. None the less, she knew quite well that she would never marry Giles Pomeroy...even should he ask.

After being acquainted with him for eight years, and thinking she knew him well, she'd at last come to know his true character. What she had believed to be his sterling qualities had now been tarnished to faults.

She felt like a flighty fool, changing her mind as quickly as the wind shifted direction. Her inconstancy mocked her. Yet with her self-reproach came a sense of relief. She knew now that life with Giles would have been dull, tiresome and demanding; she would have given her all until the light within her guttered out.

The sound of voices from the next room pulled her from her thoughts. She covered herself and slid down in the water as she recognized Sommerville's agitated voice. Peeking over the side of the tub, she saw that he had turned away and was facing the outer door.

"You must pardon my intrusion, Thea," he said. He sounded embarrassed. "I did not mean to take you unawares. But matters in this house have come to a sorry pass, and I found I had to seek your counsel."

"What troubles you so?" Thea asked.

Sommerville raised his hands, as if words couldn't encompass the entirety of the problem, then he dropped them to his sides. "Alys needs... Dash it, she needs a husband! Your sister is one of the most capable women of my acquaintance. Her talents are varied and numerous. And, of course, as your sister, I hold her in the highest esteem. But she has set the servants against her. And this afternoon, after being gone for a considerable time, she returned in Duncan's arms, igniting a blaze of gossip below stairs that is likely to burn for a month. Our butler told me that she had dampened her petticoats to a shocking degree. My valet advised me that a quiet wedding could be arranged. Then my impudent, prosy third cousin comes to me to petition for Alys's hand. What's to be done?"

Alys sat up and listened intently.

"Do you desire Giles to be more closely related to us?" her sister asked him.

"No, confound it. I don't wish to give him an excuse to camp forever on my doorstep. But if Alys's reputation is threatened, then we may have no choice in the matter. Besides, for years she's had her cap set for him. I daresay the whole family expects them to marry sooner or later."

Alys dropped her head in her hands.

"I've always been grateful," Thea said, "that you had the wisdom not to let others' expectations influence your judgement."

Sommerville chuckled. "My dear, it is you who has the greater wisdom. Through your kindness I am always much more clever than I can actually lay claim to being. You help me to ignore the obstacles and only view the heart of the matter."

"You give me too much credit, sir." Thea soothed the baby as he began to fuss, then let him suckle at her other breast. "The servants are undoubtedly happy with their gossip. Cousin Giles is certainly content with his rock. But will Alys be content with Giles? We must ask ourselves whose happiness is most important in this matter."

"My dearest wife, I don't give you enough credit. You are a wonder." Sommerville turned then so that he at last looked directly at Thea. His expression softened as he openly watched her nurse their child. "Forgive me, but I must tell you that I've never seen you look more beautiful. I don't think I have ever told you how lovely and good you are...or how much I rely upon you...or how grateful I am for all your sacrifices.''

"I've made no sacrifices. With a willing heart, I came as your bride and I remain as your wife." She put the sleeping baby into the cradle.

"Perhaps we shouldn't risk having any more children. I nearly went mad when I thought I might lose you during your travail." He knelt beside her. "Thea, you're my life. Your happiness is my happiness. I shall love you beyond death. But, while there is life in me, let me show you—every day—how I love you."

"Oh, my darling Edmund," Thea murmured, "I want to give you four more children and four more after them. We mustn't be afraid anymore." The silence that followed was fraught with passion.

Alys eased out of the water and closed the door. Guiltily, she conceded to herself that she should have given them their privacy long before. Yet to have missed a word of their declarations would have been a great loss. It was *momentous*. She had never heard her sister call Sommerville by his Christian name.

She dried herself and left the dressing-room as soon as she was decently clad. As she hurried down the corridor to her bedchamber, Giles stepped out of his room, as if he'd been awaiting his opportunity.

"Miss Champion, I must speak to you about a very private matter." He searched his pockets, but came away empty-handed. "I had something very particular I wished to say, but I cannot find my notes."

"I should be happy to delay our conversation until you find them."

He stared at her damp hair, then allowed his gaze to slide down her dressing-gown. "No, I dare not wait. A scant hour ago I was struck by your feminine attributes. Suddenly, as if inspired, I had an idea that would not normally have occurred to me. I don't know why I didn't think of it before today, but you would make a man an excellent wife, Miss Champion. Your housekeeping skill is well known in this establishment. And I would venture to say that a man's *every* need could be supplied by a lady like you." He dabbed the moisture from his upper lip. "I want you...as my wife."

Here was the fruition of all her schemes! But instead of being the delight of her life, his proposal was excessively distasteful.

Nevertheless, her family seemed to await the announcement of her betrothal to him.

"Of course, I know what your answer will be," Giles said, a touch of smugness coating his tone. "You're a spinster, and far from being a fool. But I know that as a lady of sensibility you will want time to consider. I shall wait on you in the morning."

CHAPTER ELEVEN

An hour before dawn, Alys kicked off her coverlet and cast her nightcap on the floor. She'd spent most of the night waking every so often, ready to rise and tell Giles to go to the devil. But how would she explain to her family that she had rejected his offer?

A spinster, long on the shelf, simply did not turn down a proposal made by a man who was revered by his family and fellows. She would be thought very odd indeed.

As she dressed, she considered her future carefully, and reached a certain resolve. It mattered not if she had to sit on the shelf until her thirtieth year and beyond, she would marry for love or not at all. And she would never again succumb to the sort of foolish hero worship she'd bestowed upon Giles. Though she might be criticized, she could not wed a man merely for the convenience of her family. If she became known as eccentric, so be it. Perhaps she would take up philanthropical endeavours.

Though the house still slumbered, she felt full of renewed energy. She decided to make a casual inspection of the lower rooms to see if they were being properly attended to by the servants. She would offer her recommendations to Thea.

As she went down the stairs, she noticed that the hall below was faintly illuminated, making it lighter than the rest of the darkened villa. Coming to the last step, she saw that the front door stood open and that a lantern sat on the stoop. Beyond the door was a dray and a stout work-horse. The shadowy forms of two men appeared round the cart. They seemed to be securing something on the conveyance.

Signore Senusi stepped into the light and stood still, as if suddenly aware of her presence. "Miss Champion," he said in a startled voice. He waved his hand behind his back and glanced over his shoulder. "Did we awaken you? You are no doubt wondering what we are doing down here so early in the morning. It is easily explained. Ah...I, ah...that is, *we* are, ah...taking the Stone...back to the museum, of course."

"Is Mr. Pomeroy helping you?" she asked. She didn't really want to see Giles now, but she was quite prepared to give him her decision.

"No. He thought that it would be safer if only Baka and I took the Stone away. The servants cannot be trusted, and he suspects a traitor in the house. Please, tell no one that you saw us."

Alys walked through the doorway and raised the lantern to examine the dray. Baka seemed to be trying to conceal himself behind the large pole he held. "Are you quite sure that the relic is sufficiently secured?

How odd. I was sure that Mr. Pomeroy would want to bid his rock farewell.''

Smiling, Senusi took her by the hand and led her back into the house, then said, "His presence would draw unwanted notice. I am to act on his behalf." He kissed her wrist. "How lovely you are in the lamplight. Have you never wanted to escape from your world and visit foreign lands? Have you never yearned to feel the sea breeze caress your white skin? Have you never longed to see the land of the ancients? The world is yours. I give it to you."

The fire in his eyes alarmed her, but she found him too nonsensical to be considered dangerous. "Your gift is too great. I cannot accept it."

His eyelids closed and he pressed her hand to his chest. "You are the night's sweet nectar. I thirst for you. I must drink of your sweetness."

"You must let go of me."

"I could take you," Senusi said, seizing her arm in a rough clasp. "But if you come willingly, our delights would surpass even my dreams. Come with me to London…and beyond." He pulled her to him and, as she pushed away, he began to murmur strange words she could not understand.

His manservant stormed in, whispering words similar to Senusi's, though his tone was far from loverlike.

Alys glanced from one to the other. The dark memory of hearing that dialect came back to her. With a shiver, she stiffened in Senusi's hold. Of course, she should have listened to Duncan; he had tried to tell her.

She stared at Senusi with a look of distaste. *He* was the amorous thief!

He was again trying to make love to her and attempting to steal the Stone. And she'd stood by like a simpleton, letting him do it once more. She was a greater dunderhead than Giles!

Pulling out of her captor's grasp, Alys ran for the stairs. She heard someone overtaking her, but dared not turn to see how close he was. Before she set foot on the third step, she was clouted on the head and she stumbled forward, falling in a heap.

ALYS HELD HER HEAD with one hand as she groped her way across Duncan's bedchamber. He was the first one she'd thought to go to after regaining consciousness.

"Who's there," he said gruffly. He sounded only half awake. "Stand, or shall I fire."

"Duncan, it's Alys."

"Blister it, my girl, what the deuce are you doing in m' room?" He lit a candle and raised it high. The bedclothes had fallen about his waist. He sat there bare-chested, glaring at her, and with a pistol beside him.

For a moment, as she stared at his hairy, muscled chest, she forgot her reason for coming. Curiously, she began to feel very warm from the inside out. When her cheeks felt burning red she turned away and braced herself against a chair.

She cleared her throat. "Duncan, I—I need your help. They've taken the Stone. If we hurry we can catch them. You were right: it was Senusi and his servant." She listened for some sound indicating that he was taking action. "What are you waiting for?"

"Would you like me to dress before you? You stand between me and my breeches."

Edging towards the door with her face averted, she said, "I'll fetch my pelisse."

"You needn't. You shall stay here," he said sternly.

"No, I shall come with you. Senusi told me where they are going."

He was silent for a moment. "Very well, but leave no note behind for the servants to discover. I want to return you with some small part of your reputation intact. If we hurry we'll be back before they know we're missing. Meet me in the stables."

She hastened out the door so that he wouldn't hear her irreverent laughter. Meeting him in the stables seemed the most likely way to ensure her ruin. Then the memory of him sitting in bed bare-chested took her unawares and sent her speeding to the safety of her room.

She was composed at last when she quickly descended the stairs a short while later. He was waiting for her at the door with his greatcoat slung over his arm.

"Does it always take you this long to don a cloak? I've already harnessed the horses. They're a quick-stepping pair, so we'll make good time. Are you quite well?'' he asked, taking her by the arm and leading her out to the curricle that awaited them. ''Did those varlets hurt you?''

She had bathed the lump on her head, but it was the cooling of her senses that took the longest time. Brazenly she coloured the truth and claimed that her injury had caused the delay.

He then insisted that she stay behind.

Casting him a determined look, she put her foot on the carriage step and hoisted herself up. Once seated, she draped the lap rug over her and waited expectantly for him.

''Alys, I know I'll live to rue this foolishness.'' He took his place beside her, then expertly took the reins and flicked them. ''I'm not doing this for Pomeroy.'' In the grey light of dawn they started down the gravel drive at a smart pace.

''Neither am I. But I feel responsible for the theft. I keep thinking of all the things I should have done instead of the foolish things that I did do.'' She touched the bump on her head. ''I've been hoodwinked! I *shall* have justice! Can't we go faster?''

''We could if I knew in what direction to point us.''

She grinned guiltily, quite sure he would have guessed. ''Go towards London.''

Without a word, he turned the horses at the lane and then at the main road leading to Town. As the sky lightened, he slackened his hold on the reins, letting the pair quicken their pace.

Not many milestones were passed before they caught sight of the dray, moving steadily along. Senusi idly held the reins and seemed almost asleep on the seat. Baka glanced behind him, then grabbed the whip and cracked it over the horse's back.

"Don't let them get away," Alys cried. "Only seven more miles and they'll lose themselves in the outskirts of London."

With a good-natured smile, Duncan said, "You mustn't worry, my dear. I'm thought to be something of a Whip. You must allow me to manage the pair and use my own good judgement."

"But...they're getting away from us."

"Not for long. Perhaps you noticed, as I did, that one wheel on the cart is wobbling. 'Tis in danger of coming off. I don't want to push them into doing something foolhardy. We must wait for our moment."

Alys looked at him and asked, "Are you hunting them?"

He laughed. "How well you know me. Now, hold on. Beyond the bend ahead the road widens." With a minute flick of the wrist, he cracked the whip over the horses' heads, and they instantly stretched into a full gallop.

Clutching the side of the curricle, Alys prayed for a smooth road.

As the road widened, the sporting rig drew alongside the dray. Baka grabbed the end of his whip and swung the handle at Duncan's head, knocking his hat off. He tried lashing Duncan, who turned to use his shoulder as a shield for Alys. In a moment the pair shot by the single work-horse.

Duncan urged the pair on until they were a good distance ahead of the cart. He then slowed them and drew them to a halt, guiding them until they stood blocking the road.

"Alys, get down and get off the road." Duncan jumped from the curricle and stood facing the on-coming dray. He drew a pistol from his greatcoat and held it ready.

Sliding from the rig, Alys hurriedly took shelter behind a tree. It looked as if the dray would not stop.

Baka whipped the horse again and again. Then he seized the reins from Senusi and, by what seemed the force of his will, made the horse charge ahead. He seemed intent upon driving over Duncan.

With pistol raised, Duncan stood his ground.

Alys closed her eyes, then opened them. "No!" she cried.

Careening wildly, the dray hit a rut. The wobbling wheel bounced off, and as the axle struck the ground, the cart veered away from Duncan. The harness snapped and the horse bolted from the dray. The lurching cart slid off the road and bounded over a rough stretch of ground. Senusi was pitched off, and Baka held on until the cart flipped over.

Alys ran to Duncan and he caught her to him. They clung to each other. At last he set her away from him and, pocketing the pistol, left her to see how the two men fared.

"They are likely to be hurt," she said, coming up behind him. "You may need my help."

"They may be dead," he stated, looking at her grimly.

"I shall not swoon."

He took her hand in a bracing clasp and silently led her over to the first man.

Moaning, Senusi clutched his arm. When he tried to sit up, Duncan gently assisted him.

"His arm appears to be broken," Alys whispered. "He needs a physician." She knelt beside the injured man. "Signore Senusi, be still and rest."

"I cannot rest until I know the fate of the Noble Baka," Senusi uttered, then fell back.

Duncan left them and began to search for Baka. "He's here," he called from the other side of the overturned dray. "And he lives, but he's unconscious. It appears that he struck his head."

Senusi struggled to get up. "I must see him. He cannot die in this cold land. The gods would never find him. Help me, please."

Seeing his determination, Alys helped him to stand and supported him as he made his way to Baka. He berated himself with every step. She tried to placate him, but he would have none of it.

"I mocked the Roll of Fate," he said, "and now...I must pay. I thought myself better than my people, but I am worse."

"Who are your people?" she asked.

Holding his arm, he stood straight and raised his head proudly. "I am an Egyptian." When he came to Baka he fell to his knees. "He is Most Noble of the Noble. He is the leader of our secret royal guard."

Duncan glanced from one Egyptian to the other, then he looked at Alys. "You wanted justice. Shall I go for the constable? Do you want their necks stretched?"

Presented in that manner, justice became less appealing to her. "Shall we hear them first? Then we can decide what's to be done." She knelt beside the unconscious man, then looked in her reticule for a vinaigrette. Though little used, it seemed potent enough when she held it under her nose. If only it would stir Baka to wakefulness.

"Baka may not live to be heard," Duncan replied.

"I am to blame," Senusi said, hanging his head. "I used the Roll of Fate unworthily. I told the Noble Baka that we were to tarry when, in truth, it said to take action and seize the moment. I wanted to seize a moment with Miss Champion. I suited my own desires, and now my commander lies dying. I shall be hanged. Fate now mocks me."

"Tell us why you came here," Duncan said.

"I swore an oath of secrecy, but now all is lost. If Ra does not take my vitals, the buzzards will. I am a doomed man. Never again will I know a woman," Senusi said, sounding the saddest yet. "What have I to live for?" Bit by bit he recounted his meeting with

Kamose and their sore trials since coming to England.

"A fascinating tale. You should put it in a book," commented Duncan. He frowned. "Now, we must decide what's to be done with you."

"It matters not. The Roll of Fate has decreed our failure. I have shamed my father. I have done my duty, as much as my weak flesh would allow, and I can do no more." Senusi cast himself on Baka's chest, begging his forgiveness.

Baka coughed and moaned. His eyes fluttered open. He gazed at Senusi, then his glance wandered to Duncan and Alys and his eyes widened with alarm. "Who are these strange people?" he whispered to Senusi. He looked about and sat up suddenly. "What strange place is this? Why have the gods put me here?"

"Noble Baka, we are in the land of the English," Senusi said, appearing as alarmed as Baka. With a questioning gaze, he looked to Alys for an answer.

"Perhaps the blow to the head has caused him to forget," she said, glancing to Duncan for confirmation.

The Noble Baka pulled his coat together and shivered. "I wish to go home. This place is much too cold and sunless."

"The gods have been merciful," stated Senusi. "I vow to Ra that if he will save us from death by the rope I will give up my pursuit of women. I will settle in Egypt with just one." He sighed wistfully. Then, with the look of a sad-eyed dog, he gazed at Duncan beseechingly.

"What do you say?" Alys asked Duncan. "Is it to be gaol or freedom?" She and Senusi looked at him expectantly.

CHAPTER TWELVE

As THE SUN ROSE over Green Hill House, it wasn't a cock that greeted the new day, but a man's shrill cry. The anguished wail was akin to that sound a man makes upon receiving a mortal blow. The entire household spilled out of their beds to discover the source of this disturbing cock-a-doodle-doo.

They found Mr. Pomeroy in the hall, berating himself and walking in circles as he wrung his nightcap. His dressing-gown hung open and one toe poked out of his stockinged feet.

"Send for the constable! It's gone," the scholar sobbed, casting himself on Sommerville's shoulder. "How will the Society ever forgive me? A priceless antiquity lost forever! I shall never show my face to my fellows again. Banishment is what I deserve!"

Sommerville glanced around. "Where is everyone?"

After gazing about, Giles's grim aspect brightened. "What brave men! Signore Senusi and his manservant must be giving chase to the thieves. Our heroes will bring the Stone back, never fear."

"Where are Alys and Mr. Todd?" Thea asked, as she stood at the top of the stairs. She clutched the rail and cast her husband a worried look that beseeched action.

"Do not fret, my love. If Alys is with Duncan, she will come to no harm."

Nanny Jinks pushed her way forward through the flock of servants that had gathered. Though she staggered to a chair and collapsed, she appeared sufficiently recovered from the grippe. With an air of importance, she declared dramatically, "My lord and lady, she's eloped! Miss Champion has forsaken her good name for a few fleeting moments with a man."

"Eloped," Sommerville exclaimed, disbelief carrying in his voice. "Before the christening of her godson? What utter nonsense!"

"I've been betrayed!" Giles uttered in disbelief.

"I saw them quite clearly from my window in the attic," Nanny Jinks stated. "She and Mr. Todd crept out of the house just before dawn."

Emma, with Charles in tow, stepped forward and said with equal assurance, "My lady would never elope. She'd only be wed in a church, like me and Charlie."

In a superior tone, the nanny retorted, "They left in a sporting carriage. She clutched his arm shamelessly."

Thea came down the stairs, looking thunderous. "Sommerville, this is not to be borne. Get this liar out of my sight. That a servant of mine could so malign my dearest sister is unforgivable." She pointedly glared at all of the servants. "You shall see what befalls one who speaks evil of my kin.'' She turned to the butler. ''Cast her out. I will not have her in my house!''

Nanny Jinks's stunned expression gave way to tears. ''Oh, my lady, you cannot turn me out. The dowager said you would never...'' She was silenced by the unified stares of Lord and Lady Sommerville, who together presented a formidable face of authority.

With a new respect for their master and mistress, the servants filed out and, with close-mouthed obedience, began their daily tasks.

Giles shuffled off, saying he would seek comfort among the only ones left worth trusting: his books.

A few hours later, Betsy, Gaby and Nelly lined up behind the low hedge of the kitchen garden. They wanted to witness their good fortune as Nanny Jinks departed in a dogcart.

When the conveyance at last disappeared from sight, Betsy led her sisters in a series of huzzas.

Their cheers continued as they saw their Aunt Alys and ''Uncle'' Duncan slowly coming up the gravel drive in a wobble-wheeled dray. The girls' shouts of joy attracted the attention of their parents.

From an upper-story window, Sommerville leant out with his arm about his wife. ''By Jove, Duncan, how did you come by the cart? Our recently dismissed nanny swore that you left in a sporting carriage, heading north for the Border.''

Alys, dusty and wind-blown, gave Duncan a sidelong glance. They exchanged a look of comradeship. Their adventures would probably never be fully recounted, and this knowledge gave her a sweet sense of distinction, for she'd shared something with him that no one else ever would.

She wondered, though, how he would explain away their long absence. She knew that she was too tired to contrive the salvage of her reputation. And she hoped that Duncan would not feel compelled to do anything for the sake of honour alone.

"Ned, old fellow," Duncan called up to Sommerville, "send your footmen out. We've brought back the Stone... and we had the deuce of a time getting it here. Would have arrived sooner, but the dray needed repairing and then we had to gather together enough men to load the blasted rock." He tactfully omitted that they had also taken Senusi and Baka to a physician, then seen them on their way.

Sommerville laughed and hugged Thea to him. "By the sound of it, you must have a grand tale to tell us. Come up. My girls can guard the Stone until it's unloaded, can't you, Betsy?"

She beamed proudly. "Yes, Papa."

Shoving his way past the servants who'd begun to give assistance, Giles stumbled to the dray. He bypassed Alys in favour of the Stone. "She's returned! And without a scratch. It's a miracle." He clasped his hands together. "But...where are Signore Senusi and his faithful man?"

"They were unexpectedly called back to their homeland," Duncan said. "We shan't be seeing them again."

Giles sadly shook his head. "I daresay it was because of his wife...though I don't recall that he actually said he was married. Senusi had a dreadful time concentrating on his work. His mind was greatly occupied by a female...or two or three females." He gazed off toward the horizon. "He was a man of mystery. I shall miss him." Sighing, he turned his attention to the unloading of the Stone.

Duncan eased himself off the dray and held up his arms for Alys. He looked at her with a twinkle in his eyes.

She put her hands on his shoulders, feeling the strength within him, and waited for him to lift her down. As he swung her off the dray, he held her above him for a moment, just long enough to give her a searching look.

Alys felt her heart quicken. She wanted to tell him many things—loving things that she'd kept to herself. She'd been too prideful and stubborn to concede them before, but now they rushed through her, demanding to be uttered.

He retained his hold upon her after he set her down.

Every fervent, loverlike emotion within her pounded against her chest, clamouring to be released. She knew that he had captured her heart, that it was his if he wanted it.

She gazed up at him, about to speak. Yet the words refused to come. Deep within, she sensed a furious tug of war taking place. Her managing side seemed to insist that she assert herself and do the declaring, while the new-found, gentler side of her desired to be wooed and wanted to experience the pleasure of being asked.

As she stood there quarrelling with herself, she looked up into his deep blue eyes and, in an instant, nearly gave in to her managing side. She wanted him. She couldn't imagine life without him.

A secret sort of smile played across his face. And he appeared about to speak.

It was then that the clatter of an approaching carriage drew everyone's attention. The first of the conveyances arrived, bearing the guests expected for the christening. The Dowager Viscountess Sommerville, accompanied by some insignificant relations, descended in grand style. She brushed past Alys as if she hadn't noticed her.

"Mr. Todd?" the dowager asked in a supercilious tone. "By your appearance I must conclude that you have come from a revel that lasted all night. You are not at all the sort I would want for the godfather of the young heir." She pushed aside the butler as she entered the house. "Sommerville! Sommerville, what has been happening here?"

THE LAST CHRISTENING PRAYER was uttered and those who'd attended reverently filed out of St. Mary's Church. Since the late afternoon had turned brisk, Sommerville ushered his wife and his newly named son, Allister Duncan, to a waiting carriage. The words of felicitation would have to keep until the reception at Green Hill House.

The new order of things at the house became apparent as the dowager presumptuously prepared to board the viscount's carriage. With a good measure of tact but firmness, Sommerville led his mother to the next carriage and offered her the company of the rector and several notables. He then helped his daughters into the coach with their mother.

Everyone who witnessed this turnabout marvelled at it, but Alys was the only one who questioned it, quizzing the person she thought most responsible for Sommerville's new demeanour. "Duncan, what miracle have you wrought here? How did you get Sommerville to take back the authority in his house?"

His candid look of perplexity appeared genuine enough. He paused for a moment as he escorted her from the churchyard. "I did nothing," he stated simply. "Believe it or not, there are gallant souls who rise to the demands of the occasion." He tipped his hat as they passed by a group of acquaintances. "Sommerville saw the opportunity and his success with it was his entirely. Remember, nothing becomes strong that is never allowed to struggle on its own."

Placing her hand in Duncan's, Alys lingered before stepping up into one of the other carriages. She gazed at him in the same bemused way that she had as they fulfilled their duties as godparents during the christening. So much still remained unspoken between them.

"My dear," Aunt Etta said from her place inside the coach, "do not dawdle. McVicar will take a chill in this draft." She tucked the lap rug more securely about her, then up to the dog's chin.

After taking her place next to McVicar and her great-aunt, Alys lapsed into a ruminative silence. She could feel Duncan's gaze upon her as he seated himself across from her, but she couldn't make herself look up to meet it.

The line of carriages made a stately procession as they wended their way to Green Hill House, which was but a short distance from the church. Though their progress was slow, to Alys the wheels seemed to turn all too quickly. She felt the time that remained for her and Duncan was slipping away. Now that the Stone was about to be returned to the Museum and the christening was behind them, he would no doubt soon depart for his home in the north country.

Faced with this prospect, she fought the strong impulse to cast herself into his arms. It mattered not whether her great-aunt and McVicar were witnesses to her shameless display. She only wanted to be held by him.

"McVicar!" Aunt Etta cried, holding a handkerchief to her nose and fumbling for her device. "You cur," she mumbled. The air in the coach was soon overpowered by the scent of jasmine. "Would you children mind walking the rest of the way? McVicar is having a rather nasty spell."

After being set down, Alys drew the collar of her dark red pelisse up about her neck, then wandered ahead of Duncan. She meandered along the path to the river. Though the wind was brisk, her cheeks felt warm and flushed. She knew what she wanted, but couldn't quite voice her desires.

Overhead, the swallows played in the breeze, and Alys marvelled at their carefree existence. What did they know of expectations and longings?

She could see the rooftops of Green Hill House as they drew near and knew that their time alone would soon end. Glancing back at Duncan, she wondered why he was so silent.

She bit her lip as her steps slowed. The force within her that had always taken command now yielded to a small voice which seemed to whisper sage advice. The little voice told her to relinquish control, to trust Duncan completely.

She glanced at him as they left the path and set foot on the lawn that surrounded the house. Resolving not to take another step until he spoke, she stood still and waited with trepidation for some sign from him.

Slowly Duncan circled her, then stepped back to consider her more fully. She sustained his scrutiny as it stretched from moments to minutes.

"Alys," he called simply, bidding her to come to him.

She looked at him quizzically, wondering what he wanted of her, but she moved to him with unhurried steps. She stopped, a pace away from him.

"Closer," he said, his expression stern.

Her little voice whispered that now was not the time to be stubborn. Her spirit of command demanded that she have him come to her. In the end, she ambled up to him in a leisurely manner, then laid her hands upon his chest and raised her face expectantly.

"Miss Champion," he said, putting an arm about her, "you are quite intractable. 'Tis for this reason that I've stolen the march on you." He smiled at her look of incomprehension and, having put her off her guard, he kissed her in an unhurried manner. He drew deep from her wellspring of emotion, leaving her leaning against him for support.

"Before the christening," he said huskily when at last he could continue, "I made certain arrangements with the curate. On Sunday next, the banns will be read. Should you have a strong objection to our nuptials, you may voice it then."

She eased back in his arms and gazed up at him, waiting for more. She would forgive his high-handedness, but she would have her declaration.

With a twinkle in his eye, he gathered her to him. "Alys, I want everything that is mine to be yours. Will you share your life with me as I want to share mine with you? You are in my mind...my soul...my heart. You've become a part of my life I would be loath to lose." He kissed her again, conveying a strength of passion which rendered her powerless to utter a word. "I cannot go on chasing you forever. Have you I will, make no mistake. For, my dearest girl, I love you." He gazed at her with such longing that tears came to her eyes.

She blinked away the tears and tried to smile. "I never cry." But the onslaught of her unleashed emotions could not be checked. She clung to him and wept happily on his shoulder.

Duncan kissed her ear and whispered, "I've been hunting for you all my life, Alys. Would you become my wife? Say you will marry me."

"I will," she murmured, then sniffed.

He offered her his handkerchief.

When she at last looked up from drying her face, she smiled saucily. "I will marry you...if you can catch me." She sprang away from him and led him on a merry chase which ended in capture and a sweet embrace.

Above them in the house, Betsy, Gaby and Nelly watched with their noses pressed against the glass of a window in the Great Room. Their eyes widened when the couple kissed.

"Mama?" Nelly called to Thea who was seated close by. "Mama, what sort of game are Aunt Alys and Uncle Duncan playing?"

"They're playing hare and hound," Betsy said with a giggle.

Curious to see what his daughters were gaping at, Sommerville eased away from the felicitations of his guests and gazed out the window. His reaction to what he saw brought a flock of inquisitive onlookers.

Alys and Duncan's displays of affection were witnessed by all. Each deep kiss was remarked upon. For better or worse, their troth was pledged, and by nightfall their engagement would become the latest on-dit in London.

"I thought that's the way the wind blew," Aunt Etta said with satisfaction. Then, casting her terrier a stern look, she said, "McVicar, if you do, I shall never forgive you. *Faugh!*" In a moment she was waving her device about, clearing the spectators away from the window. She watched them flee, then winked at McVicar.

Out on the lawn, as the sunset began to ripen, Alys and Duncan made their way up to the house. His arm was about her shoulders to give her warmth and because he liked the feel of her by his side.

"I believe in short engagements," he stated candidly.

"I've had my bride's clothes ready for many years," she retorted with equal candour.

He glanced down at her with a look of amusement. "St. Mary's has been reserved for our nuptials one month from today."

"Must we wait so long?" She nestled against him. "Duncan, I daresay you've yet to instruct me in all the arts of the hunt. I'm quite willing to learn whatever else you'd care to teach."

He kissed her slowly, thoroughly, and then murmured a seductive, "Tally-ho!"

JAYNE ANN KRENTZ

A two-part epic tale from one of today's most popular romance novelists!

Dreams
Parts One & Two

The warrior died at her feet, his blood running out of the cave entrance and mingling with the waterfall. With his last breath he cursed the woman— told her that her spirit would remain chained in the cave forever until a child was created and born there....

So goes the ancient legend of the Chained Lady and the curse that bound her throughout the ages—until destiny brought Diana Prentice and Colby Savager together under the influence of forces beyond their understanding. Suddenly they were both haunted by dreams that linked past and present, while their waking hours were filled with danger. Only when Colby, Diana's modern-day warrior, learned to love, could those dark forces be vanquished. Only then could Diana set the Chained Lady free....

Available in September wherever Harlequin books are sold.

JK92

COMING NEXT MONTH

#81 THE UGLY DUCKLING by Brenda Hiatt
Miss Deirdre Wheaton was in a pucker. She had
fallen heel over ears in love with Lord Wrotham but
learned, much to her dismay, that in order to follow
her heart, she would have to abandon her soul.

#82 THE ABSENTEE EARL by Clarice Peters
One year had passed since Viola Challerton, Lady
Avery, had been deserted by her husband of a mere
two hours, the Earl of Avery. She had not expected
Richard ever to return, but when he did, she found
that little had changed, except for herself!